SKY LIGHT RAIN

Judy Darley was born in 1977 and grew up in Thornbury, near Bristol. Her short stories, flash fiction and poems have been widely published, and read by the author on BBC radio, in pubs, caves, and a disused church, as well as at literary festivals and charity events. Her debut short story collection *Remember Me to the Bees* was published in 2013. Find her on Twitter @JudyDarley.

Sky Light Rain

JUDY DARLEY

Valley Press

First published in 2019 by Valley Press
Woodend, The Crescent, Scarborough, YO11 2PW
www.valleypressuk.com

ISBN 978-1-912436-23-1
Cat. no. VP0143

Cover illustration by Judy Darley.
Text design by Jamie McGarry.
Edited by Tess Dennison.

Contents

To my mum Pauline, who showed me the imagined landscapes hidden behind the real ones, and to my dad Philip, who taught me that adults need stories just as much as children do.

Sky Light Rain is a collection of short stories and flash fictions examining aspects of human existence, our relationship to nature and complex behaviours towards one another.

Part one is *Sky*, touching on what binds us together while simultaneously giving us the courage, or the push, to overcome our fears.

Part two is *Light*. It explores the darkness within ourselves, and how we can come through it to find our own light. These tales take the form of a series of journeys, escapes and reunions.

Part three is *Rain*, drawing together a selection of water-inspired tales prompted by explorations of pain, beauty, and resilience.

Some tales soak into one another, with the rustle of wings in one ebbing into the fluttering pulse of the next. Family connections swim throughout – a reminder that however far we travel, some connections remain, to our past selves as well as our future hopes and fears.

Part One

Sky

Untrue Blue

As children we would go flying at night. You were always the instigator, shaking me awake then unlatching the window to let the night creep cool and bright beneath our pyjamas, under our skin. I'd edge out first, blinking in the sweep of orange-tarnished sky, beneath the faint stinging stars.

You'd crawl out to crouch beside me on the sill and take my hand, eyes laughing in your face, and we'd dive head-first into the air, down and down. Till, at the last possible moment, you'd surge us both upwards with a great kick of your legs.

Sitting here, on this bench on Brandon Hill, wrapped in your old green jumper, I can't help thinking of those times. The city glimmers in the valley below and it looks like it's been laid out for me, just as it did when we flew together. I still love the way this landscape rises, into hills and towers and bridges straddling gorges, always striving to get closer to the false blue of the sky.

You last brought me to this spot on a summer afternoon that made my skin prickle and melted ice creams into sticky pools along the park's steep paths. Children and dogs raced one another, and we watched grown men play Frisbee with a competitiveness at odds with the sweetness of the day.

Cabot Tower was still out of bounds then, covered in scaffolding that glinted like something precious. You reminded me how Mum would take us up there when we were small, your voice breathless as you told me, "The view from up there is even bigger than this one, Tia."

I didn't remind you how it used to make me reel, how all that space and sky above and below us would make me damp and pale with fear.

I've been avoiding Brandon Hill since you left me behind. With my back to the tower, I feel it stretching up into the sky; my skin tightens with the fear it will glance down and reach for me.

Our worlds seem to intersect most strongly here, and I haven't felt I've had the strength to resist it, withstand the fierce, mineral smell of that other place, your place.

It isn't that I've tried to forget you. That would make no sense – you're part of me, as much as you ever were. But I've made a conscious effort to move on. I've even started seeing someone, a boy. A man, I suppose, though he seems more open, more vulnerable than most adults tend to be. His name is Jack, like the Giant Killer. His eyes, when he looks at me, shine with hope; he gazes at me and lets himself see a future, whereas, I think, you looked at me and saw only our past.

Would you be jealous of Jack and the relationship we've forged in your absence? It's because of you we ever met, so you've no grounds to resent it.

I first fluttered towards him – a moth caught in a draught – in a cramped room that reeked of grief, guilt and stale coffee. They paired us up like a sick kind of ultra-specific dating service, but what we had in common rather than a love of sunsets, country walks and a GSOH was that we'd each lost someone. His heartache was for his dad, and coupled with the grief was a cold anger: a rage at his abandonment.

I can relate to that. Why didn't you take me with you? I'd have overcome my fear of heights once more for the chance to travel there by your side.

I remember seeing that flint of desertion spark in your eyes after Mum left us, before we found ourselves displaced, 're-homed', in grey buildings where monstrous foster creatures lurked.

In the support group meetings I can't bear to listen to the tales the others tell; I sit and watch them, ears only half tuned in, sifting their sorry stories into fairytale versions of the world – false blue after false blue. There's Maria Muffet whose daughter was fatally bitten by a poisonous spider; poor Jill, whose brother fell while rock-climbing; Rita Hood, her sister killed by a ferocious dog; Gretel, whose brother simply disappeared, may not truly be dead. She leaves a trail of breadcrumbs for him every night, hoping he'll find his way home.

Actually, I think that last one may be real; at least in her mind.

It's springtime; crocuses and primroses litter the grass, vivid as childhood toys. Maybe that's what's drawn me back here after so long. I'm too warm in your jumper, but I don't want to take it off, not yet. There's a freshness in the breeze that makes me picture us playing tag here, hide and seeking, Mum laying out the picnic rug as though preparing for a fairy feast.

Remember when she was in the last stages of her illness, how she made us wipe our tears and told us not to be sad? She promised to wait for us in the other place, where sunny afternoons last forever and you can swim through air as easily as water; the place through the hillside and behind the waterfall where everyone is young and healthy forever. A land where no engorged giants wait for night, ready to advance.

Thinking of you, I smell water against stone; feel the chill of miniscule droplets in the breeze. You're on the far side of a waterfall and I can't even hear its roar.

I've begun to dream of you returning to me, tapping on my window and begging me to climb outside and join you. Leaving my Giant Killer snuffling through his own dreams, I slide onto the sill, shivering as the air pinches me.

You take my hand and we're out there, in the thin, frail sky. The river murmurs far below as we trawl past spires and office blocks, above the mud-thick banks where I used to be certain crocodiles slept, through the gorge, and up to the bridge, its spatter of lights mirroring the stars.

Your hand is cold in mine, like it doesn't quite belong there, and when I pull away, you laugh. "What's wrong, Tia?"

Then I'm falling, silently, wind rushing past, without your upward kick to save me.

Why could I never fly alone? Were you the only one with that power, and I truly only ever your passenger?

Jack's dreams are haunted too: his dad appears beside him, blank-eyed, cavern-mouthed; leaking river-water from every orifice. He was found sodden and submerged – a castaway shopping trolley, wheels rusted and mud-crusted. Jack trembles when he tells me, and his eyes leak too, but when I hold him I find I can make him feel safe.

I don't tell him my dreams, though I let him hug me, stroke my back. He's determined to love me, despite this being a relationship built on losses – trying to fill a void neither of us fully understands.

Recently, my dream shifted; instead of flying to the bridge, we swooped to Cabot Tower, stood on the parapet over the shadowy inclines of Brandon Hill. You gripped my hands, whispered, "Tia, will you?"

"Will I what?"

"Will you jump?" You laughed in my face, and I sensed you were mocking me and my fear.

For a moment I felt the tower had got hold of me; clasped me tight against my will.

So I did it, I gripped your hand and we leapt high and far, soaring through a sky so thin we broke through it to another sky, where droplets sang in the air and blazed silver against our skin. Mum was there – or a version of her – eyes whirling like they would consume me. It was that sight rather than the plummeting sensation that shocked me back into bed, into my body.

The scaffolding has been removed from Cabot Tower, peeled back, stripped away, leaving it naked and phallic against a too-blue-to-be-true-blue sky. You taught me about the falseness of the colour, revelling in breaking my heart a little as you explained that the sky isn't truly blue.

"Really, it has no colour," you said, "no colour at all." Giving me cause to doubt everything my senses told me as fact.

Like the giant who climbed into my bed at night in our foster home, the hulking creature that forced its way beneath my pyjamas, under my skin. That must have been false, mustn't it? A recurring nightmare I had to wash away in the light of day.

I didn't want to tell you in case you decided to play the role of avenger, stabbing our foster-dad in the eye with a serrated grapefruit knife over the breakfast table.

I never wanted to be avenged, or rescued. I just wanted it not to be true.

You always tried to be my hero, but I couldn't let you do that. I needed to find my own way forward. It never occurred to me that you might be the one who needed saving.

I'm not afraid to scale the tower now, ascend the worn stone steps with narrow slits to let the light in. I stand at the top surveying our city, my city, and feel secure. The air is thick today, swollen with the scent of newborn flowers, no chance of you reaching through and grasping me, dragging me into your place.

Last night I woke mid-dream, mid-step, sleepwalking to the window. Jack had stopped me with one warm, strong hand on my wrist as I reached for the sill. He led me back to bed, let me sleep with the comforting weight of his arm across my back. Pinning me down, but not trapping me; keeping me from danger.

Standing at the top of the Cabot Tower in the sunshine, I take your jumper off, hold it out at arm's length, let go. At first it plummets, and then it unfurls, catches the air as though it's about to take flight. It descends right to the base of the tower, lands beside a homeless man sleeping there. A gift.

Weaving Wings

THE BEST TIME is when we have an hour outside and can run and race like we're still on our way. I pretend that I'm running to my mama and that this is all a game.

We are told we are being cared for by the Department of Health and Human Services. I think I would prefer to be a bronze-winged woodpecker or Yucatan wren, like the ones Mama showed me in our yard back at home.

Those of us old enough to know our alphabet write secret notes to our mamas in the minutes when we're meant to be finishing homework. I doodle birds in the margins so Mama will know I haven't forgotten.

None of us has found a way to send our letters, but we keep them under our beds as testimonies to hope.

We write in our home language, although we learn new phrases in English each day. We don't know where our parents are, so we don't know if they're learning the new words as well.

When we are told it's time to play, they bring out armfuls of bright yarn. We each grab a handful of strands in green, white and red, for before, or red, white and blue, for after.

We weave each other friendship bracelets to stand in for wings. We play tag with our eyes leaping to the sky, watching birds we saw at home glide high above our fence, telling each other they must fly over wherever our parents are too, and we smile to see how they cross borders without anyone taking them from their flock.

Woman and Birds

EULÀLIA DOESN'T MEET me at Barcelona Airport as promised. I tell myself that she must be busy with our daughter Ocell, and catch a taxi into the city instead. The driver has a kind face; I tip him more generously than I normally would and feel a stab of something like self-righteousness. See, I'm being good even when Eulàlia is not.

Eulàlia has rented me an apartment close to Plaça de Catalunya. She invited me to stay at the family home, but I declined – with dignity, I thought. I'm an independent woman these days, after all.

It's immediately clear that my ex has double-bluffed me. The apartment is basic, verging on dilapidated, shielded by scarred wooden doors that cue me to ask the driver, *are you sure?*

Yes, he is sure. I key in the code Eulàlia sent by email and ascend the steep steps to the third floor as directed. The apartment is a single room with a narrow, lumpy bed from which I can gaze directly into the microwave. So intimate.

Perhaps I'm being paranoid, I tell myself. Perhaps Eulàlia has no idea quite what she's rented on my behalf. But as I turn to dump my case on the bed I see a splash of colour, a painting pinned above the meagre pillows. It's one of Eulàlia's own, showing a woman on the back of a giant blue-feathered goose. There's a sense of movement in the artwork – the woman's coppery hair streams behind her in the breeze as the duo fly through a green and silver sky. It's almost identical to the mural that made up one wall of Ocell's nursery.

My mobile cheeps. The message reads: *Welcome to Barcelona! Ms Eulàlia and Miss Ocell invite you on a Treasure Hunt! Do you accept?*

I sit down. The mattress springs squeak. So here it begins. I sigh, text back: *Yes, I accept.*

There's a pause, then a message zings in. *Great! Please be sure to wear blue and red.*

I unzip my case. All I have in blue is an old faded t-shirt of Eulàlia's that I sleep in. I pull it on; add a black skirt and a pair of red hoop earrings. Fantastic, I resemble a gangly ginger fortune teller.

My phone chirps again. *Clue 1: Blue Route.*

I stare at it blankly, key back: *???*

Another long pause, and then a response: *Look for the sign of the sun in Plaça de Catalunya!*

*

In the square, fountains burst upwards in the heat and a flight of stairs rises, stacked upside down against the blue. I spin slowly, allowing the sun to pool on my skin, and spy a sign topped with an emblem of a red-lashed oval that could be a child's drawing of an eye. It's the Barcelona Bus Touristic sign. The Blue Route bus has just arrived.

I settle on the top deck of the bus and send a text. *On board, now what?*

Patience! comes the answer. *Enjoy the ride.*

The bus drives onto Passeig de Gràcia and passes Casa Batlló, with its balconies shaped into gigantic carved molars. I recall Eulàlia telling me that the trio of modernist buildings it belongs to are known as the 'Block of Discord', and permit myself a wry smile, thinking of the discordance our own little trio represents these days.

My phone squawks. *Clue 2: Seek the fearsome thing.*

I glower at the screen. The clue's phrasing is familiar; it nags at me. Ocell and I moved back to England so I could take care of my dad after he had a stroke. He vowed to guard Ocell from the monsters she believed lurked under her bed. The fearsome things, that's what he called them.

After he died, she was inconsolable, afraid to sleep, afraid to be alone. "The fearsome things will come and eat me!" she whispered.

She's seven now, and regards herself too old to be afraid of goblins, dragons and the like, but still…

We're nearing Parc Guell, home to Gaudi's famous salamander. I exit the bus and enter the hilly gardens. The woman at the entrance to the monuments area looks at me strangely, and then waves me straight through without asking to see a ticket.

I pause in the Plaça de la Natura that was intended as an open-air theatre, surrounded by swirling benches mosaic-ed with shattered ceramic. Was it deliberate, Eulàlia sending me to this space after the times we slammed crockery to the ground to punctuate our discontent?

No one has ever been able to infuriate me the way she can. Before we met, I was a steady, sane individual. She drew my passion to the surface, both good and bad.

An image of her fingertips tracing their way up my ribcage makes me shiver.

I scowl and shove the memory away, striding down the steps to the Hypostyle Room. Sweeping columns give the impression of a cathedral, a forest. I linger for a moment, drinking in the tranquillity.

Another sly memory steals in. I stood here surrounded by enchanted stone trees and melted as Eulàlia confessed her love to me. Our breath had formed haloes in the frozen air, but I felt gladness ignite within me. That was our beginning, or almost.

I raise a hand to my cheek, wiping away a tear in confusion.

Tourists throng around the inelegant, amiable-looking salamander – not exactly terrifying, but still…

A man approaches. He hands me an origami goose. I unfold it to find a note that reads, *Clue 3: Red Route.*

I return to Passeig de Gràcia, where the Blue and Red bus maps intersect. As I sink into my seat I glance upwards. Ocell stares down from a balcony jutting out from Casa Batlló. She smiles and waves as I twist towards her, mouth agape.

I hear my mobile chirrup.

Stay on the bus, the message reads. *You'll get your little goose.*

I grimace. This trial has gone on long enough. The clues tangle with my emotions more than Ocell could comprehend.

Eulàlia, though, I'm sure Eulàlia knows. She's never got over me taking Ocell with me when I returned to England, just as I haven't forgiven her for retreating when my dad was ill. We've formed an uneasy alliance over the past year, enabling us to interact when required for Ocell's wellbeing. But the wounds remain, sore as blisters in the sun.

The Red Route's journey winds uphill; the terrain shimmers. I listen to the recorded commentary, learning things about Barcelona that I've forgotten or never knew. It reminds me how much I've missed this city.

We ascend Montjuic and I notice a tower in the distance – a sweep of graceful calligraphy in white.

Another text appears: *Clue 4: Fire transformed to communications.*

I think for a moment, listing possible synonyms for fire in my head: sun, star, heat, flames. I consider communications, and glimpse again the tower that pierces the horizon – the commentary states it was built to transmit the 1992 Summer Olympics to the world.

I disembark at the Olympic stadium.

The space it inhabits is immense. A fountain pours into the square below, and the square below that. Yellow columns climb into the sky, and the tower soars above it like something carved from ice.

I first came in wintertime, when Eulàlia was still my language teacher, my guide through the Catalan tongue. I'd found her through an advert pinned to the university noticeboard; we'd been meeting at coffee shops and tapas bars. She offered to bring me to see the tower, and as I stared up at it in awe, leaned in fast.

Our first kiss.

Light flashes from the tower. I wonder if I'm supposed to find a way inside, but glancing down to the lower squares, I see two distant figures, an adult and a child, wandering towards a distant shady area. It's difficult to discern more than outlines in the brightness, but the child looks dark haired to me, fine-boned, bird-like. Surely my Ocell.

I run down to find them, but it's further than I'd guessed. By the time I reach the shadows, they're long gone. A paper goose remains, rocking in the breeze. I scoop it up; unfold the winds. My fingers tremble.

Clue 5: Wire transformed to flight.

Each clue so far has led me to another landmark in my early days of loving Eulàlia.

I shake my head, frowning.

In the year we've been apart – me in England, her here in Barcelona – we've withdrawn to the extent that we now barely speak. Only Ocell keeps us in each other's lives. She's spent the whole of August with Eulàlia – it's time for me to take her home. Ocell, my little goose, is the treasure at the end of the trail. I tell myself to keep going for her sake.

I've visited the site of our first kiss, and the place where we meandered in our early love-drunk days.

On our first official date Eulàlia took me on a picnic at the top of Montjuic. We travelled via cable car.

Wire transformed to flight...

I walk down the road, passing Fundació Joan Miro where we'd to go to admire the Catalan artist's eccentricity. Together we'd giggle like loons over the way it seemed every other artwork was titled *Woman*, *Bird*, or *Woman and Bird*.

The attendant in the cable car booth grins and refuses my euros. He hands over my ticket along with an origami goose. I half-smile back and enter the confines of the next car, feeling my stomach swoop as it lifts me into the air. For a moment Eulàlia's painting alights in my mind, the one showing a copper-haired woman riding a colossal goose. She painted the woman to mirror me, and the goose to represent our new baby daughter.

In Catalan, Ocell translates as bird. It seemed so romantic at the time – only later did I think to ask, *why is the goose carrying the woman? Shouldn't it be the other way round?* She'd laughed softly, and said, *but you'll carry each other.* It's true. When my father faded from us, Ocell was the one who held my hand, mourned him with me; motivated me to pick myself up and carry on.

Perhaps, I think, perhaps she's the one orchestrating this painful trip down memory lane. I think about the message that instructed me to wear blue and red. She knows I still sleep in Eulàlia's old t-shirt – the lone blue item in my wardrobe.

I undo the origami. Eulàlia's familiar scrawl simply says: *Sorry.*

For what? For letting me down two years ago? Or for leading me on this wild goose chase through the city where we lived together? Sitting in a clear bubble above Barcelona, I feel the sense of loss well up. Just overtired, it's made me emotional, I tell myself. I scrub my face with one hand and raise my eyes to the scenery.

A cable car bobs slowly past, travelling in the opposite direction. I see our daughter mouth *Mum* as she waves.

My phone cheeps with a text from Eulàlia. *You ok?*

I sigh and laugh. Text back: *Having a merry old time. You?*

A pause, then: *We miss you. Don't worry. We are nearly at the end.*

At the peak, I emerge into sunshine. Gigantic ants march the walls overlooking the port. I'm far from the city streets, far from wherever my estranged wife and child will soon arrive.

I spot something in the grass, perhaps blown off the wall. Another goose. I spread its wings. Eulàlia's message reads: *Don't be infuriated, please.* Of course I'm annoyed – why shouldn't I be? But *infuriated* seems an odd choice of word.

The memory unfurls with a flick. After our picnic, she suggested we stroll down to the port. She claimed it was a short distance and beautiful all the way. The serenity of gardens had soon given way to graffiti-ed paths. My sandals bit into my heels; I could feel blisters taking shape. Eulàlia implored in her awkward English, *Don't be infuriated, please.*

I nod to myself; set off down the hill. My phone tweets as I glimpse the harbour boats.

Clue 6: Anger transformed into love.

That could mean any one of our arguments, but one in particular comes to mind. I was five months pregnant with Ocell and had just told Eulàlia that my ageing father wished me to return to England. Eulàlia had been enraged by the idea, and I'd been appalled by her anger. I stormed off into the crowds, losing myself amid holidaymakers. I'd come to a halt beside two sculptures – La Pareja, by Chilean artist Lautaro Díaz Silva; La Pareja means the pair.

Eulàlia taught me the nuances of that word, how it could mean a couple, a partner, or the relationship between your left and right shoes. She told me people would smile at us and murmur, *hacen una bonita pareja*. When she'd caught me up, when I'd agreed Barcelona was too addictive to leave, I sat sandwiched by the two statues while Eulàlia photographed the three of us. The space between the bronze statues was so tight I almost had to be prised free.

Their impossibly long legs resembled tails, and they had no arms with which to hold one another. They were like survivors of some disaster – merpeople ripped with force from their sea; fish out of water. Just as Eulàlia was when she visited England and our fights grew uglier than ever. Ocell crouched and listened on the stairs, hearing our cries as shrieks of battling dragons.

But afterwards, when she left and tranquillity descended through clammy autumn air, we both missed the heat of her fire.

*

Ocell may have begun this treasure hunt, but Eulàlia has directed each move – I'm sure of that. For some reason the thought makes me smile.

A scrap of paper in the shape of a goose rests on the knee of the merwoman. I open it and see the words: *Clue 7: Woman and Bird*. I nod, unsurprised. Parc de Joan Miró, where this sculpture stands, is where Eulàlia proposed marriage eight years ago.

I walk through the city, gazing at the sky between buildings and watching the vast, abstract figure claim the view ahead. She's crowned by a small moon representing the bird. There's a bounce in my step, despite my tiredness. I know with certainty that Ocell and Eulàlia will be standing beside Miro's monumental woman, hands clasped.

Shaped from Clay

ON THE LAST day of term I allowed the children to bring in toys to play with. As her choice, Ebie brought a bag of whitish clay dug from the river that ran through the village. It wasn't quite what I'd had in mind, but she looked at me with those silver-blue eyes, and I couldn't think of a reason to say no.

I instructed her to use the area by the sink where we washed our story-time milk bottles, and watched from the edge of my concentration as she began to pound out air bubbles. Her hands dug into the clay, pushing into the flesh of it like it was something she was attempting to throttle the life out of, or palm life into.

At story-time, she refused to come and sit on the rug to drink her milk.

"Join in, won't you, Ebie?" I tried. "Come and listen to the tale of the raven who stole the sun. It's a good one."

"I know it already," she told me. "My nanna says if you replace the word sun with love or food or power, you'll have every human story ever told."

I settled down with the class and read them the fable while Ebie carried on kneading the clay.

The history of Ebie's family was written deep into the village's soil, whereas I was a newcomer, living just beyond the boundaries and only recently moved up from England's south.

Jonas, the school's caretaker, was another outsider, arrived from the opposite compass point to mine. More than once we'd sat together in an abandoned orchard overlooking the streets, sharing whisky he'd brought and watching the moon come up. Dandelions glistered orange amid the greenery, and later in the season ambushed us with parasol seeds. When I called them grenades I saw a strange sickened look cross his face and wanted to bite the words back out of the air.

He liked that my name was Pearl; said it reminded him of the moon at its fullest. "Those are the safest nights in the village. When the moon's just a slither, be careful." He knocked a mouthful back and grimaced.

I let loose a laugh that died as he glowered.

"I mean it, Pearl. On those nights, stay indoors if you can."

"All right." I grabbed the bottle and tipped the fierce liquid into my throat. After I finished coughing, I folded myself into the space between his arms, seeking the heat at his core.

Before the night was out, my lips found a scar on his abdomen that unwound an unwitting question. His answer – "Afghanistan" – stilled my tongue from asking more.

He whispered his belief that the small parish was a battleground, eons old, where every resident shared common ancestry. "Don't let your guard down, Pearl."

His words smelled of peat and orange peel.

He was in my classroom on that last day of term, replacing a windowsill catacombed by woodworm.

"Watch that 'un, Pearl." He nodded to Ebie's sleek head. "I've seen other bairns here with that look about 'em. Never ends well for anyone."

His words made me shiver, but I chided him with my eyes and did my best to suppress the dread that clawed my insides. I'd only ever wanted to teach, and for all their rosy cheeks and plump bellies, there was a starved look about the children here that made me feel they needed me.

When the others brought their empty milk bottles to the sink, Ebie asked if she could wash them out.

The clawing sensation inside me heightened, but I couldn't think of a sensible reason why she shouldn't be permitted. "Of course you can wash them," I said, and observed from the side of my face as she added a trickle into each from the tap, pouring the milk-fogged, spittle-threaded water over her clay. Some splashed onto the floor, forming murky puddles at her feet.

Then she started to shape her clay, as clouds swung past the classroom windows and the sky deepened from blue to violet.

Little Lessie Alster wandered close to watch as the lump began to change under Ebie's hands, drawing out into flanks, fetlocks, withers, a sweep of shoulder and a tangle of mane. The nostrils she'd sculpted with her thumbnail flared wide and my head jerked as I thought I heard an equine harrumph.

"Wanna help me say the chant?" Ebie asked, and Lessie nodded, quick and eager. Together they murmured a litany of words I couldn't quite grasp, Ebie speaking first and Lessie echoing each syllable just a fraction behind. They built up the sound like the river after a storm. The skin of my neck twitched.

"Ebie, I'm afraid we don't have a kiln to fire your creation," I said.

"Worse luck for you, Miss."

"It means the clay won't harden up and be strong."

She flashed me a gap-toothed smile. "It's as tough as I need it, Miss."

A pulse leapt in my throat as I tried to smile back.

The sun eased between clouds, casting skeins of light throughout the room, and the horn that rose from the clay unicorn's brow glittered.

Things felt unsettled throughout that break from school. Whenever I visited the village market to buy jams simmered with quince or windfall pears, there were fresh rumours in the air.

"Have you heard, Pearl?" asked the stallholder each time she wrapped in new jar in paper. Tales flooded me of kids infected with measles, chicken pox and more archaic diseases, including, she confided, something that caused boils to blister their tender skin.

One pupil's older brother had disappeared without a trace during a camping trip. In the morning his sleeping bag was empty, though his boots remained secure inside the zipped-up tent. "Should have known better than to camp out on a sickle moon night," the stallholder said, shaking her head.

An unearthly yawl met me when I came home late one night from seeing Jonas. Bones brittle inside my flesh, I edged towards the kitchen, and discovered my cat choking on a spray of feathers.

I dragged it from his jaws and found myself holding a raven's blueblack wing.

My cat was never the same after that: eyes slits of mistrust whenever I tried to come near.

Poor Jonas crashed his car and fractured a leg.

"What happened?" I asked when I visited him in hospital.

"Swerved to avoid hitting something," he said, face tense. He grabbed my wrist with one rough hand and described a large white animal that glimmered from the dark – "a deer or a horse."

I pushed away thoughts of Ebie's clay creature; the way it seemed to shine. My breath heaved and I snatched my arm from his grasp.

"My own fault," Jonas said, both hands open now as in surrender. "The moon was just days old."

He was still laid up when the new term began.

The traffic was so snarled up that I reached school when the bell had already rung. With fumbling fingers, I unlocked the classroom as children lined up behind me. The door swung inward, releasing the stench of sour milk, a stiff metallic tang and a reek of burnt flesh.

A dead raven lay on my desk, its one wing spread wide, the throat bent back at an angle that made me need to swallow. Children trailed past me warily through a haze of dust that drifted like ash.

Ebie was not among them.

Outside, a sudden wind shook the trees, and the classroom swarmed with shadows. In the gloom, the clay unicorn shone – its horn a twisted javelin. I heard myself hiss through my teeth, speared with a sudden anger.

Lessie took one glance, hooked a stray milk bottle from the sink, and swung the vessel wide.

The horn shattered under the blow. Shrapnel showered the floor, a pearly liquid streaming after it.

Lessie turned and gazed at me solemnly, her eyes glinting silver-blue. "Things will be better, now, Miss."

Knotted Rope

A Tale in Three Voices

MEG

Rita and I and our two volunteers count with care on the nursery steps. Seventeen, eighteen, nineteen… That's everyone, isn't it? A whole flock of little ones. Every child wears a fluorescent tabard and clasps tight to the length of blue rope, tiny hands wrapped around knots tied like memories.

We get the kids to sing as we walk, high voices lilting into the chilly air. The sound sends shivers racing up and down my spine – reminds me of being that size myself with the world a big clear bubble around me. I look at the houses we pass, wondering whether anyone comes to the windows to witness our twice-daily parade. I would if I was one of them. Wouldn't be able to resist. A few curtains twitch, but no one shows themselves.

The gates to the old cemetery are large and heavy, propped open like the entrance to a forbidden place. Some of the parents find it odd that we bring the children here; they think it morbid, but I disagree. There's far more life than death in it – the gravestones tipped and tripped about by ivy, trees heaving with squirrels and birds. I've heard people tell of roe deer wandering between the tombs.

Sometimes I think I glimpse other creatures in the foliage, eyes and teeth glinting, but I keep that to myself.

Dogs are meant to be on leads here, but more often than not they run loose, pausing to stare at us as we approach all together – a noisy people-cloud. I wonder if the children envy the canines' freedom; the dogs certainly seem bemused by our dinky people on strings.

We march the pre-schoolers along leafy paths, avoiding the worst of the mud and pointing out buds on branches, robins and magpies. Occasionally, one will forget themselves and skitter off, drunk on the possibilities. But they're tiny enough that we're able to speed over and scoop them up. For most, the threat of missing storytime keeps them gripping onto their knot.

A new one started last week – Andrew. Just moved to the area with his jagged-edged mum. He's walked with us each morning, clutching onto the blue rope with the others. He doesn't join in with the songs. In the cemetery I watch as he gawks at the woodland. There's a light in his eyes that makes me wary. He's meek, or rather, quiet. Easy to confuse those two. Does as he's told, silent mouth pursed, but I can see that his mind is swooping away.

An animal runs in amongst us, black and silky – a hairy Scots terrier. The children crouch with their free hands outstretched as Rita flusters at them to be careful, saying it might bite. She fusses too much. The dog grins at us with interest, nose snuffling around ankles and knees, making some squeal with a skim of joy.

The sky is clouding over. "Better head to the nursery, Meg," says Rita. "Shall we sing a cheerful song?" Rita is large and rosy and forthright. Her bluster bothers me at times, but there's a kindness beneath.

We pause outside the cemetery gates, counting fast. Sixteen, seventeen, eighteen. That's everyone, isn't it? Rita starts the children singing about sparrows shouting from eaves, and we stride along the narrow street as quick as the shortest legs will allow. We'll be at the nursery in time for a story and a drink of juice for each child.

RITA

It's almost half eleven. Meg is supposed to be supervising tidying up while I stack the dishwasher, but I'm suddenly conscious of her in the kitchen doorway. Her breathing is loud and fast, and she's grasping the knotted rope like she's afraid to let it go.

"Whatever's the matter, Meg?"

She opens and closes her mouth a few times, gulping air. "Rita,

I've checked every corner, every space I can think of, and I'm sure…" she breaks off, pebble eyes blinking madly.

"Sure of what?" I prompt, impatient.

"One of the children is missing."

My lungs tighten in my chest. It has to be a mistake, I tell myself sternly, holding in the panic that's boiling its way from my toes to my head. "Oh, I don't think so, Meg," I say.

"We left one behind," she whispers, "in the cemetery."

"We went with eighteen, returned with eighteen. Didn't we?"

She shakes her head. "We made a mistake. The new boy, Andrew. We… We forgot him."

My armpits prickle. "Let's have a peek, shall we?" I say, "Just to make sure."

I follow her into the main room; try to see it all at once. Fail. Resort to looking at it in sections – naming each child in turn as I see them: Olivia, Amelia, Harvey, Toby, Henry, Muhammad, Eva, Aisha… They're clumped throughout the space, two here, three there, one playing under the windowsill.

I repeat the process, fighting to keep my breaths from flapping around my ribcage.

I can't see him.

He's definitely not here.

"Have you checked the lavs, Meg?"

She nods. "We miscounted, Rita. Thought we were wanting eighteen, but we wanted one more." She makes a peculiar face, as though she's attempting to suck in her lips through clenched teeth. "Do you want me to call the police? Andrew's mum'll be here soon."

I hesitate.

The nursery door swings open and a woman walks in.

It isn't Andrew's mum.

"Not a word," I hiss as the woman greets her child with a hug and gives us a wave. "Check the lavs again, will you? And get the volunteers to run back to the cemetery. Just in case."

She frowns, but does as I say.

I stand motionless; watching parents arrive, collect children and leave. Andrew's mother turns up when most others have been and gone. She's harassed, overtired, possibly undernourished. It's an appearance I'm familiar with, and usually means a relationship on the rocks or already in shreds.

I make an effort to pay extra attention to the children with parents like that, but there isn't always the time. Andrew's been no trouble – not acting up like some in his circumstances. Whatever they might be.

I watch his mother scan the room blankly. Meg emerges at the far end of the room, shaking her head. She blanches when she spots Andrew's mother.

"Mrs…" I can't summon her name, or even whether she's married. Her gaze skims over me distractedly. I touch her arm. "Will you come with me for a moment?'

"What's happened?" Andrew's mum asks, her high-pitched voice puzzled. She sounds like a child herself. "Has he done something wrong?"

I tilt my head at Meg to indicate she ought to stay with the children, and steer Andrew's mother through the door that leads to the office.

"Mrs…" Her name bubbles up from some dark recess and I spit it at her. "Mrs Woodrow, we've had a little mishap."

She glares at me, seeming less concerned than exasperated. "Oh, what now?"

"I'm sure he's fine, but… we're just not completely certain where he is."

I watch the mother's expression shift, become unreadable, and I need to know she's understood, so I add, giving weight to the words: "We probably need to phone the police."

ANDREW'S MUM

"Oh, for heaven's…" Exasperation bubbles through me. "That little…"

The woman gapes at me, and I know I'm doing this wrong. I

should be wailing in floods of tears, but I haven't got the energy for this.

"Mrs Woodrow?" The woman blinks at me owlishly.

"It's not the first time," I tell her. "He does this. Runs off, waits somewhere till I'm out of my mind with dread, then pops out and drinks up the attention."

The woman doesn't seem to be listening. "I'll phone the police now, Mrs Woodrow." She presses a hand to my shoulder.

I shrug it off. "Let's wait a bit, yeah? No need to bother anyone." Wish she wouldn't call me that – Mrs Woodrow. Like I'm my own mum-in-law. Ex-mum-in-law. If they ring the police I'll definitely have to let his dad know.

The other woman joins us, the mousy one who weirds me out with her pale, mournful eyes. They're extra pallid today; reckon she's the one who should have been minding him when he slipped away.

"They've all gone home," she whispers.

"Where were you when you lost him? I've got stuff to do and the sooner we find him, the sooner I can get on."

She flinches. I watch the pair exchange glances, and the one in charge says, narrow-mouthed, "We were on a ramble, weren't we, Meg? Such a pretty day. The children love it, don't they?"

"Outside?" I ask. That changes things a bit.

"You said he's gone missing before," she says.

I nod. At a shopping centre on the outskirts of Bristol, he had the entire place sealed up, police and security scouring every corner before he uncurled in John Lewis' haberdashers. Almost gave a sales assistant a heart attack.

Outside is worse…

"The primroses are flowering," the mousy one says. I can tell she means to be reassuring. "It's beautiful in that cemetery."

The owlish one makes a soft noise of concern, or rebuke.

"We keep them safe!" The mousy one pushes something into my hands – a strip of blue rope with knots at regular intervals. "We get them to hold onto the knots and they each have a little fluorescent tabard. Andrew's a good boy, I bet he's still wearing his."

Words rush from me like the red rising after a slap. "You've lost my son in a graveyard?"

I let them phone the police then, an iciness gripping the place where the top of my ribcage meets. The owlish one tells me they've already sent two volunteers "just to be sure."

When the officers arrive, they ask if I have a picture of him. I show them the one on my phone and wonder if they're judging me for not having a proper one – an actual printed photo. But surely all they need to know is that they're hunting for a lost child, a three-year-old boy, alone in a cemetery.

My throat aches like I've tried to choke down something far too large.

We hurry to the cemetery and it's this massive place, wild and overgrown. The volunteers turn up – anxious, empty-handed.

I turn slowly, blood pounding in my head. He could be anywhere.

The world wavers around me. I hear myself panting; a wave of heat washes over me. Someone takes me by the shoulder and steers me until I'm sitting on the edge of some old tomb. My fingers grip the edges of it, nails digging into lichen.

"Breathe," someone tells me, like that's not all I'm trying to do.

I overhear one police officer mutter to another: "Shame it's not a girl."

"Excuse me?" A voice rattles through the air. "What difference would that make?"

"Oh, none, nothing. Just, little girls tend to carry things, hair slides…"

I open my eyes a crack and see the officer pointing to a broken clip on the side of the path. The pink paint is peeling away; it's spotted with rust. "They're more likely to leave a trail."

The mousy woman from the nursery glares at him. "If you're any good at your job you won't need a trail, will you?"

A different officer squats beside us, gluing on a soothing smile. "What kind of places does Andy usually hide, Mrs Woodrow?"

"It's Andrew, not Andy." Somehow that seems important. I grip my knees. "Don't know. Anywhere. Everywhere…" I gesture to the trees, bushes. It's early afternoon, but the place is thick with shadows. "I'm going to have to tell his dad, aren't I?" I murmur, wondering whether a text would do it. No, I'm better than that. Better than he was to me.

"Maybe we can get one of the police to call him," the mousy one suggests.

I glower at her. "Think they've got something more important to do, don't you?"

Reinforcements arrive and we fan out, searching in earnest. We're covering the whole area. Around me all I hear is the noise of strangers shouting out my son's name. If he's still here, he must have heard us, surely.

If he's still here.

It's as though the sky is revolving about me. I have to stop, lean on a tree for a moment; head low.

"Are you ok, Mrs Woodrow?" asks the owlish one.

"Give me a bit a space, won't you?" It comes out sharper than I intend, but she backs away.

I think of my boy and rest my cheek against the trunk, trying to get into his head. Blinking, I see the blue brown green of ferns and trees. Feel the coldness of the air – he's been out here for hours. I picture him huddled somewhere, with the drag of thirst in his throat, pins and needles in his feet from hunkering down for so long.

A bird screeches; I flinch.

I think he might be scared, like he got whenever his dad and I used to argue, like the time his dad threw a glass across the living room and it smashed into the wall. I found him in the hallway cupboard that day. He was wet through from pissing himself.

I think that hiding gives him a moment of peace away from the grown ups pulling him in different directions. The urge to take off comes over him, big and thumping in his stomach, telling him to escape. But then, I bet, the impulse goes and the only thing he wants in the world is to be found.

We lost Andrew overnight once. It turned out he was in the

cellar, creeping deeper and deeper into the dust and the darkness in response to the sound of us ripping the house apart above him.

It'll be the same here, I know it, hearing us thundering towards him. He'll disappear deeper, afraid of being caught and scolded. Being in trouble yet again.

I think of bedtime and how the stories ease over him, make him attentive and calm even after the stormiest of days.

The search party is well ahead of me now. I wait until the squirrels have gone back to their errands in the trees, and I begin to tell a story, out loud. I don't know what to say at first, but I remember the blue rope the mousy one showed me, and the knots tied into it.

"Each knot acts as a magic force-field," I say slowly, "keeping whoever holds it safe."

I think of the caged expression Andrew wears sometimes, how trapped he often seems to feel. I try again, and this time the knot is an egg, "a dragon's egg, and only the heat of a child's hands wrapped around it can help it to hatch."

I swear I can feel his gaze on me.

I pull the sensation towards me, and keep talking, low and soft. I kneel down like I'm hoping to attract a deer to feed from my hand.

And there he is, behind me – so close that I can feel his breath on my neck. Relief spins through me.

"Is it true?" I hear him ask.

"Maybe," I say.

Andrew shuffles through leaf litter until he's beside me. I turn my head so I can look at him. No injuries, as far as I can tell, though he has smudges of earth on his chin and cheeks. I ask if he'll take my hand so I can stand up without overbalancing, and he does, his fingers sodden from being sucked.

He's still wearing his fluorescent tabard, like the mousy one said he would be.

He's a good boy, my Andrew.

I bend down and pick him up, holding him on one hip, legs hanging down. He's heavy, but it feels so good to have him in my arms. I walk to where the grown ups are gathered, and everyone exclaims in amazement. I hug him tight, burying my face in his shoulder.

When I look up, I see the mousy one watching me. The gleam in her eyes tells me she knows what I know. My boy may be clinging tight now, but his fears are merely resting. Under his surface, worries coil around each other like an anxious nest of dragons.

Somehow I need to find a way to soothe those creatures and keep my Andrew safe.

Two Pools of Water

THE HOTEL HAS stood empty for seven years, or eight. In the humid island air, lichens and moulds bloom along the balustrades. Almost every valuable item, from linens to sinks, has been stripped out by creditors. The carpet remains – squelching under our sneakers. In one en-suite a claw-footed bath still stands; its curve of porcelain laced with grime.

My sister Estella leads me to a balcony. The twin lakes show beyond, half-shrouded in cloud. With the sky overcast, the green and blue are harder to see. She tells me the fairytale I've heard a thousand times before, of the shepherd and the princess, embracing on the bridge and weeping through their farewells. "Her green eyes made the emerald lake, and his blue eyes made the sapphire one," she says. "He cried more, which is why the blue lake is so much bigger."

The truth, of course, is that the sapphire lake looks blue because it is bigger; that's why it reflects the sky when the smaller one shows only its chlorophyll-dense depths.

"Ssh," Estella says, not wanting me to spoil it. Even when I don't speak she can see the criticism in my eyes.

She wants me to be a child forever.

I like to kayak on the emerald lake with my friends. When we pause to breathe in the quiet, I lean over the water to see the fertiliser-plumped beads of algae spooling like distant asteroid clouds.

I wonder if that's similar to what Mum sees when she looks up or out. Wherever she might be. No one talks about why she left, but I think she couldn't stay and not see whatever's out there. I picture her boarding a boat in the harbour and not caring where it carried her, so long as it took her far from here. I imagine her arriving in a cold country on the far side of the ocean, where cats stalk brown birds instead of flick-tongued lizards. I bet before she packed up and went, the idea of the world burned in her blood until she couldn't be still.

Or perhaps I just think that because it's how I feel: full of hunger, full of want. It's the buzz that makes me run extra hard, jump extra high when playing basketball on the school court; makes me want to spin round and race my sister down the rickety hotel stairs, to fling myself into the arms of the first boy who craves me.

"What colour were Mum's eyes?" I used to ask, when I was small and knew no better.

And Estella would shrug; shake her head. "How should I know? It's too long ago."

If I'd been older when she went, I know I'd remember.

Dad has brown eyes, like the rest of the islanders.

Like me.

"The village boys will bring you here soon," Estella warns. "They'll try to win you over with this story, then play the shepherd's role. Don't forget, the princess had more to lose. That's why she cried less. She knew her father was wise to break up their romance."

I've heard this before too. Estella began telling it to me as soon as I got my first menstrual bloods. That was more than two years ago and the boys have yet to make their move.

I'm tired of waiting.

"When did they try it with you?" I ask, imagining how it might have been. I wonder whether the carpets were dry then, if the smell of rot lingered less. I paint a night sky backdrop, the stars glittering bright.

The image in my mind glows.

Estella is staring at me, frowning. I think she sees the yearning tickling beneath my skin.

I match her questioning stare, and think back to when my sister was my age, seven years ago, or eight. How I woke in the night to hear her voice thinning the air as she argued with our father.

The moon was already high in the sky, yet she'd just come home.

From behind our bedroom door, I heard her shout: "But we love each other."

I like to think that the hotel still had its beds then, decked out in the softest sheets.

I match my sister's stare and wonder how long it took for her to agree that our father acted wisely.

Estella blinks her eyes the colour of two pools of water. I recognise the fear in them – Dad had that look after Mum left, and again when Estella found love. I take her hand in mine, lace our fingers together, and I shake my head. No promises spoken means none to break.

Apollo's Offspring

RAVEN COMES HIGHLY recommended, but despite this, something about him makes me nervous. That beak, those clawed feet, and his way of looking at Mabel and Stanley with one eye and then the other makes me deeply uneasy.

The children are delighted by their new au pair, however. I haven't heard Mabel chatter like this since before their father left. And, as my mother likes to point out, I clearly need some help. The house is a tip, discarded clothes and toys crowding every surface.

Little Stan had jam crusted at the corners of his mouth when Raven arrived, but before long I see my son accept a damp cloth from the bird's curled grasp and scrub himself clean.

Raven tilts his head to one side, indicating the kitchen door. I shrug and nod. What harm could befall them in the back yard? He bustles them outside. I hear the thud of a ball bouncing and my children's laughter.

Worse than the beak and the talons and, frankly, the fact he is a bird, is the annoying detail that before he took up childcare, he worked with my ex, Lo. Something to do with a messenger service that had the immediacy of email and the old-fashioned quality of a written letter. Sounds like a winner to me, but something went wrong. Something to do with the woman before me, Lo's innate jealousy and a mishap with a candle. Raven's tail feathers still have a singed look about them. Hearsay has it that prior to his argument with Lo, Raven's wings were as creamy as my children's curls.

Lo, my great and terrible love. We're so much better off without him.

Raven, though, is beloved in our community. He's come to the aid of many an overwhelmed parent and set their offspring on the path to righteousness. The children adore his eccentric ways. I watch him instruct Mabel and Stanley in a complicated game involving dropped leaves and pebbles, and notice happiness in their darting movements and utter absorption.

I turn away from the window and busy myself with loading and switching on the dishwasher and cleaning the counters of accumulated grime. Then it's almost lunchtime. I make tuna fish sandwiches for Mabel, egg and cress for Stan. I think about how Lo used to stand and stare at me until I'd turn with a scowl and ask him to explain himself. Sorry, he'd say, sorry my beloved. It's so hard to always be aware of how our passion will wither.

Foresight can be a curse, for sure.

I try to remember what ravens eat but can only think of carrion, or perhaps that's crows. A ham salad might cover all bases.

I go to the backdoor to call the children and Raven in, but can't see Mabel or Stan. I scan the yard, taking in the acacia and roses, the washing line and the pond. Maybe they're hiding.

Raven. I spot Raven; he's standing on the pond. For a second, I fully believe that he's walking on water, but then I see that he's treading on the spread of lily pads. His head is tilted to one side, gazing into the murk beneath.

My heart is in my throat, preventing me shouting my fright. Instead I watch, eyes aching with intent. It's as though he's searching for something. My blood seems to have set in my veins, turning me to stone. I hear myself croak: "Gar, gar!"

The water fractures, droplets ringing up and out as the heads of my children emerge.

My voice and blood are freed at the same moment and I burst forward out of the house. Mabel and Stanley are safe on the lawn by the time I reach them, bundled up in towels that Raven has rustled up from somewhere. I crane closer as they each raise a hand, passing their au pair something plucked from the pond's depths.

Raven nods, then jabs and gulps, one, two, leaving empty snail shells spinning.

You risked my babies' lives for a snack? I yelp.

He regards me in that way I'm already growing to hate: first one eye and then the other. You would rather they consume the slime themselves?

Raven explains that the snails are uncanny, each imbued with whatever the person who retrieves it needs most to thrive, to grow well and strong. Of course, I murmur, wrong-footed as always in interactions with the creatures from my ex-husband's world.

What did Mabel get? I ask. Raven regards her faintly glowing snail shell askance. Self-assurance, he tells me.

And Stanley?

Self-doubt.

My children have already forgotten their adventure, busy playing a game of hopscotch along the path. I watch them leap, wobbling first on one leg, and then the other.

Crouching to scoop the translucent snail shells into my palm causes a momentary headrush – all the world's future possibilities colliding inside my skull.

With care I stand and turn to see Raven watching over us all.

The Puppeteer

How long had it been now? Tib wasn't certain. More than one year, less than two. God, how had so much time crept by? He thought he'd get them back before this many months. Once the numbness and confusion passed, he was certain he'd be able to win Nancy over, persuade her to bring Pippa home, but it had already been eighteen months, maybe twenty. Or more…

He'd only seen young Pippa once since they left him, and that had been in the most humiliating of circumstances.

Things slid downhill after Nancy and six-year-old Pippa moved out. In an effort to reject all Nancy had accused him of; caring more about his work and the puppets than about his wife and daughter, he'd turned his back on his creations. Then, in an act of rage, as though they were sentient enough to be culpable for the ruin of his marriage, he piled the whole lot up in the centre of the lawn, set them alight.

He tried not to feel their bewilderment, not to hear their shrieks of fear, as the flames sent acrid, choking smoke into the night sky, making a dark scorched circle on the grass. Tears carved tracks down his sooty face, and he told himself he was committing some kind of sacred act; a magician's trick to bring his wife and Pippa home to him, prove how little hold the puppets had over him, compared to his love for the two of them.

But that was the business gone. His former clients found new talents, better puppet-masters; young-bloods with the power to give life to lurid factory-formed scraps of fabric that Tib figured ought to lack the power of his own hand stitched creatures. He took a job in a phone shop, wearing a suit he was ill at ease in, trying to talk teenagers into signing contracts that would lock them in for years to come. He felt like Satan's accomplice.

Each night for what seemed a decade or longer he went home

to the dingy flat and felt more alone than before he'd met Pippa's mother, because then he at least had the puppets.

It was laundry day that sucked him back in to it. A stray, freshly washed and dried sock slipping from the basket to the floor. Tib picked it up and, telling himself it was just to keep it safe while he searched for its mate, stuck it onto one hand. Naturally, his fingers in the worn grey cotton toe formed the nose; his thumb in the heel, the mouth. He should have seen it coming.

He found its mate, drew it on over his other hand, let the pair chat to one another and to him. Righty and Lefty, the first friends he'd made since his wife left. Tib felt the closest he'd come to happiness in a long time.

One day while he was performing with these two at the buskers' spot near the abbey, he saw her. Older than he'd thought possible – more years than he'd reckoned on must have slipped by without him noticing. She was with a gaggle of mates – it was one of them who noticed him with a ring of tourists around him, laughing and cheering the puppets' antics on.

"Oi, Pippa, int that yer dad?"

She'd glanced up, met his gaze, then recoiled with a force that seemed to catch at something deep inside his chest and tear it a little.

She shook her head. "Nah, don't be daft! My dad don't live round here."

He watched her slope into the crowd, head down low like she was trying to hide herself from him. Yet she'd looked him in the eye, and he'd stared right back at her.

Weeks skidded by before he had the nerve to act, let the puppets badger him into picking up the phone, leave a message with Nancy. "Tell her that tomorrow I'll be at the bar on the corner near where we used to live," he said. "Just tell her that. I'll wait all day if needs be. If she don't turn up, that's her choice. But I'll be there."

It took all his courage to leave the flat, head across town, pass the house where the burnt circle still blackened the lawn. Only the two balled up socks in his pocket gave him the guts to do it.

He found a table in a far corner where he could watch the door from, nursed his drink, nursed another, watched shadows track across the floor.

"I'm going to go home," he muttered at last. "This is stupid."

"Hang on a bit longer," Righty urged.

"Yeah, you said you'd wait all day," Lefty nodded. "Give her a chance."

"Yeah," said Rightly, then added sagely, "Give her a chance to give *you* a chance."

So he sat, he waited, as the afternoon sun sneaked in and painted the wall behind him golden, and he half closed his eyes against it, so that when he blinked them back open he wasn't sure what he was seeing was true. Standing before him, biting her lip, half the six-year-old who'd left with her mum and half the sixteen-year-old she'd become.

"Pippa." He dragged the puppets off his hands, shoving them into his jacket pockets. "Pippa, you're here."

Fascinate

I STILL REMEMBER the April when we were small and found a nest of ducklings in a hanging basket. We climbed up on the kitchen roof and scooched close to stare at them.

"Ducklings are magic, Helen," you told me. "They're so fluffy they can survive a fall from any height."

You reached out and scooped one into your palm before I could stop you. It sat there, the breeze weaving through its downy feathers. Then, grinning, you launched it with force into the air. It splatted against the flagstones below with a squelch that rang through my head. You blinked at me, and giggled.

"Oops. Don't tell, or I'll blame it on you." You slithered off the roof, kicking the tiny corpse beneath the rhododendron leaves where no one would see.

Now we're grown and sensible, but you're still my kid sister, even if you are about to be married.

You tasked me with booking the hen party. "Something cool," you said. "Something none of the hens will ever forget."

When I spotted the craft-ti-dermy classes, I knew I'd found the right thing, although the thought of it made me feel a bit sick.

Taxidermy for a new generation – desiccated chicks, mice and birds decorated with sequins and stitched into fascinators.

"Helen, it's perfect!" you squeaked as we settled down to get to work with tweezers and thread. The other hens murmured politely, loathe to own up to the horror wriggling through them.

Choosing a creature was a challenge. I watched you paw through the cadavers. "Is there a kitten?"

The course leader explained that people don't like to dismantle cats or dogs – the trend for ghoulish doesn't reach quite that far. I suppose they have to draw the line somewhere, or some bride, somewhere, will be gliding down an aisle with a baby's sweet feet curling coquettishly on her tiara.

In the end you opted for a starling, killed by a collision with a plate glass window.

I chose the smallest thing in the heap – a frog murdered by dehydration.

All had died of natural causes, none raised and slaughtered for this purpose, we were assured.

We slit stomachs, removed innards, inserted miniature glass eyes like gems.

At last the torture ended. Your fascinator was a triumph; the wings outspread as though taking flight.

On the day of your wedding you were a vision in ivory silk, your lipsticked smile so wide I felt you'd crush anyone who dared gaze at you with less than awe.

Your starling-carcass fascinator crowned you.

I watched the sky for murmurations, and wondered whether I'd speak up if one appeared.

A Blackbird's Heart

B RON WATCHES AS Nan grasps her knife and slits the deer from throat to groin, easing the flesh apart until the glistening innards slide free.

She senses the monkey's anxiety as it climbs from one of her shoulders to the other. "Hush, Caru, you're safe."

The smell of blood is sharp in her throat, not just the deer's but that of her brother's wife, Derlyn. The birth was difficult. After his first caterwauls the baby has gone quiet, exhausted by his battle to enter the world. Eyeing the infant's pink mottled flesh, Bron thinks he seems little different to the piglet that will represent him in the deer's carcass.

"What shall I name him, Bron?" Derlyn murmurs. "What would your brother want?"

"Let's worry about that later," Bron says, seeing the translucence of Derlyn's skin, exhaustion blooming around her eyes.

Her brother Caio once told her this was how their own mother died, with the effort of heaving Bron into life. She shutters the thought away. The family that's living now – that's what matters, she tells herself, and she listens as the baby sighs in his sleep.

*

"Bronwyn, tea's on the table!"

Her foster mum sounded like she'd been shouting for a while. Bronwyn uncurled and bounced on pinned and needled feet. "Coming, Pat!"

She ran up the garden and into the house, aware of Pat scrutinising her as she neared. She'd overheard Pat talking to her foster dad in low tones that week, saying: "It's not normal, Ken, a girl that age, spending so much time alone. She's been with us two years – how can I get her to open up?"

It made Bronwyn uneasy to hear herself spoken about that way. If they wanted, they could cast her out in an instant. It had happened before, with others, and she knew they'd considered it when her brother got into it with their darling daughter Deb. Craig had been fourteen then, two years younger than Deb – the one fact, Bronwyn suspected, that had saved them.

Bronwyn liked living in this house, with this family. Deb was almost a big sister to her. But now Deb had her own little one. What would they want with a moody twelve-year-old no one else bothered to stick with?

*

The elders wash the deer's organs, parcelling each up and returning it to the still warm cavity, muttering the rites that honour the animal's death.

One of the boys brings in a screeching piglet. "Here, this one's small enough."

"I'll do it," Bron says, stepping forward and lifting the monkey onto a beam. She has the blade ready.

"As you wish." Her grandmother nods her approval. "Twelve is old enough, and the new-born is your nephew."

Bron has watched this act almost as many times as there are now children in the hut. She slices the piglet's throat, abbreviating its shrieks, and catches the blood in a bowl. Half will be mixed with the birth bloods and the first gush from the deer's body; half with the broth the piglet will become to feed the mother and, through her milk, the child.

Any leftovers will go to those most in need – food is scarce after winter, and the demands of the castle dungeons never to lessen, although not all their men could have survived the freezing months.

Bron snips off the twisted tail, holds it up and whistles softly. "Here, Caru, for you!" The monkey takes it from her hands and chatters over his prize like the women speaking their incantations over the cadaver.

*

Bronwyn sat at the table, frowning as Ken slopped pork casserole onto her plate. They were cheap cuts, as much gristle as meat. "Here, Caru," she whispered, holding out her hand under the table so the tabby cat could eat from her fingers.

"Bronwyn! What have I said about feeding Calico your dinner?" Pat yelped.

"Sorry, forgot," Bronwyn said, adding a broad smile for luck. "Can we visit the baby later? And then see Craig, tell him the kid's born?"

The adults swapped glances. "Not sure your brother would appreciate that, would he?"

"He'll want to know about his son," Bronwyn insisted, and saw their expressions darken.

*

"I'll take the deer to the castle," Bron says, speaking the words she's been nursing for so long.

"You're too slender, cariad, the weight of it..."

"But I'm strong!" It's true. She's been training with the boys to build up her muscles ever since Derlyn's belly began to swell.

"Let her do it," Derlyn says, weariness thickening her words. "You know her brother would love to see her."

They wrap the tiny pig's heart in paper and place it inside the deer, stitching the wound closed. Two of the bigger boys heave the stiffening corpse onto the sleigh.

Bron cocoons herself in the shawl Nan knitted from the dense fibres of valley sheep.

"Will you watch Caru while I'm gone?" she asks the oldest of her cousins. "You know how he is when I'm not around." The monkey has been her constant companion since she set her mind to making him her own.

She strides out into the blue of the afternoon, ice crunching beneath her feet and the runners of the laden sleigh.

This time of year, this almost-spring time, is the hardest for everyone, harder still since the invaders thrust the families from their castle. When they'd tried to reclaim it, the weather had been against them – sleet winds fighting them as fiercely as the soldiers. Bron's brother led the surge and was stricken down with the rest of them.

He and his men have been in the dungeons for two winters, with their families expected to provide their sustenance, or let them starve.

The newcomers, who have their own superstitions, respect the local's beliefs; monthly conjugal visits and ritualised food preparations are permitted, the latter allowing messages to be passed with the sanctified organs. The heart of each creature inserted bears a different meaning – swine for a birth, a hen's heart for death, the tiny beater of a blackbird for love, loyalty and hope.

A monkey's heart for war.

*

Deb's new baby was far larger than a piglet, it transpired.

"Can I name him?" Bronwyn asked, reaching out one hand to pet his plump, downy cheek.

Deb smiled at her. "I already have a name picked, love. Russell, after my granddad."

Bronwyn frowned. "But what about Caio, I mean, Craig? Doesn't he get a say?"

Deb frowned. "Oh, now, Bronwyn. You know Craig's been at the Young Offenders for more than a year – do the maths!" She stopped talking suddenly, intercepting the looks her parents shot her way. "Well, you can hold him, if you want."

Bronwyn sat down in the chair closest to the bed. She let Pat ladle the baby into her arms. "I've read all the Deceangli Family books now, Deb!" She beamed over the child's heavy head. "I'm writing my own."

"Oh, well done," Deb said, busy admiring a little knitted cardigan her mum had brought.

It was Deb who'd introduced Bronwyn to the trilogy, with the heroine who shared her name. Bronwyn held the baby close. "One day, kid, you'll get to rule the kingdom," she whispered, too soft for anyone to hear.

*

Bron guides the sleigh through the snowy forest to the castle.

"I'm here to see the prisoners," she says at the gate. "I'm Caio's sister."

The guards wave her through, indifferent.

Caio blinks to see her walking towards him, dragging the sleigh over cobblestones.

"You've grown," he comments.

"Almost fully," she agrees. "How are things here?"

"Cold. Dark. We lost old Llwyd to fever."

"Spring comes," she tells him. "I heard a blackbird's song on my way here."

She sees his gaze lighten and is glad of her lie.

"No talking between insurgents and visitors!" the guard on duty barks.

Bron rolls her eyes, making her brother smile. "I bring you meat, Caio, from your wife."

His jaw tautens – he knows the code that tells him to search for the heart. He'll not be sure until he identifies it whether to mourn a death, celebrate a birth, or something else.

*

They spent so long at the hospital there wasn't time to visit Craig as well.

"Maybe tomorrow?" she asked.

"Maybe." Pat nodded. "We need to put the finishing touches to the nursery first, ready to welcome Deb and little Russell home."

The nursery had been Craig's room when they came to live with Pat and Ken. In the first months there, Bronwyn had rushed in whenever night terrors shuddered her awake – craving her brother's reassuring presence. Late one evening, she'd arrived to find her place beside him already occupied by Deb.

Thinking back, she wondered if the attention Deb lavished on her – brushing her hair, giving her hand-me downs, buying her each book in the Deceangli trilogy – had been only to keep her quiet.

She shook her head, trying to dislodge the thought. They were a family: she, Craig, Deb and the new baby. Getting them back together was what mattered.

Deb had painted the nursery walls with branches of squirrels and robins. "Deb said you can add something in the empty space over the window. Would you like that?" Pat asked.

"Yes." Bronwyn grinned. She knew exactly what to paint, high up where it could watch over the child.

*

At the hut on the far side of the valley, preparations are well underway.

"Bron," cries Nan. "You ready? It's time."

Bron runs inside the hut. Her pulse thuds so vigorously she can barely draw breath.

"I know what we should name your son," she tells Derlyn, who has the baby nuzzling at her breast. "Mwyalchen."

"The word for blackbird!" Derlyn exclaims, smiling. She reaches out a hand and touches it to Bron's. "Yes. Yes, it's perfect."

*

Bronwyn's painted blackbird glimmered in the nursery with feathers as dark as a winter's night. The bird would be the baby's guardian – keep him from straying as Craig had and prevent him from being taken from them.

She wiped her hands clean on the rag Pat had given her. The tabby cat, Calico, padded into the room, sniffing suspiciously at the paint.

Craig had never liked Calico. Bronwyn saw him kick the cat in the rear once. She'd shouted at him, and he'd laughed at her anger.

"Dad would've done much worse. Do you really not remember?" When she aimed a kick at him, he grabbed her ankle, tipping her off her feet.

"I'm teaching you an important lesson," he said as he comforted her afterwards, "You've got to be tough to survive, kid."

Now, Bronwyn picked up the knife she'd used to pry open the paint tin. It was too good a chance to show Craig what she'd learnt.

"Here, Caru!" she crooned to the cat, her breath jumping in her lungs.

*

Bron whistles to Caru, tempting him down from the rafters with early sweet berries. He chatters as he devours them: a final supper of sorts.

As an act of respect, she will close his bronze-speckled eyes when the light fades from them.

Bron scratches his head and runs her hand down his spine, feeling the thick, soft fur of his winter coat. Then she reaches for the blade at her side.

It's time to release the monkey's heart; send the message of war that will ignite the uprising that will free her brother at last.

Beyond the wooden hut, she hears the first blackbird of spring begin its lilting song.

Paper Flowers

JULIA HANDS THE yellow felt-tip to Chiara, half watching as she adds a few dots of ochre-yellow to the heart of a paper lily: pollen that will never billow free.

"What's wrong, ha?" Chiara asks, focused on her task. "You've been almost silent since you arrived."

Julia shrugs, trying to smile, but Chiara re-caps the pen, flicks her eyes towards the younger woman, insistent.

"Bianca…" Julia admits, and she snorts.

"Of course, Bianca. What's her trouble now?" Chiara's own daughters are grown up, married off, safe. Julia's eldest is fifteen, that most lethal of ages, when everything wants to devour her, and she seems hellbent on devouring everything.

"There's a boy…"

Chiara hoots. "When isn't there?" She snips the petals of a tulip a little more roughly than intended, tsks, and tidies the ragged crepe edges. "Who this time?"

"Not local," Julia admits. This is what perturbs her most. The island boys are in a semi-permanent state of arousal, it's true, but they're harmless for the most part. The tourists, with their way of flitting in and out of the islanders' lives, worry her. She was once one of them; she remembers how wide and uncaring the world outside the lake island can be, how enticing it can seem.

"Where from?" Chiara asks, frowning. Julia knows she's never travelled beyond northern Italy, but as a mother she grasps the sense of this threat.

She says softly: "American."

Chiara makes a whooshing noise, then places a wrinkled hand over Julia's. "At least he's not Australian."

As though distance is the only concern.

Julia sets aside the clutch of daisies she's been threading together and starts work on an arrangement of pink roses, wondering if Bianca will even care about the avenues of flowers for the Santa Croce festivities. Last time, she was just ten, younger than her sister Patrizia is now. Julia recalls the paper blooms entrancing her then, and how she danced with her little friends in the glow of lanterns as night fell.

Of course, Francesco was still alive at that time. If he was still with them now, perhaps he'd have stepped in this morning, forbade his daughters from boarding the strangers' hired boat.

"You want a boat ride? Go fishing with Matteo!" he might have barked.

All Julia did was remind her to look after her little sister, made sure they each had sunscreen, and waved them off on their way to Carzano's quayside.

When Julia first came here, eighteen years old and uncertain stepmother to dark-eyed Matteo, the flower-making bemused her. Francesco suggested she join the women in the squat building at the lake edge, where they sat preparing for the next Santa Croce fiesta. Scraps of crepe paper covered the table, drifted down to the floor, as they worked with scissors and lengths of wire, creating bloom after rustling bloom.

"You've already won my heart," he told her, "Win theirs and every heart in the hamlet will follow."

So she sat with them, amid a sea of baskets and vases stuffed with roses and other blossoms so realistic it seemed strange that the air wasn't thick with their fragrance.

Gradually she learnt to shape the flower petals, decipher the local language, contribute to their commentary, and ask about the motivation for devoting so many hours to a pointless, if pretty, exercise.

"We're working to ward off the sickness and death of the population of our hamlet," offered the elderly Patrizia who Francesco and Julia named their smallest daughter for.

"We do this each month, every season," another said proudly. "Then, after five years, we have enough for the next Santa Croce festival."

"But why is the festival is held?" Julia asked, although she'd read in a guidebook that it's a pay off for the residents' survival through a cholera epidemic more than 500 years ago.

The women looked blank for a moment, conferred among themselves, then an answer came back. "Fewer than 250 people live in Carzano, and each family must provide 30,000 paper flowers to decorate their allocated area." That's all. They've forgotten the rest.

"It's a dying art," they told her. "None of the younger women are interested in spending their time cutting and twisting paper into petals. Except you."

Julia smiled, felt positively noble, vowed to teach her own children the traditional skills.

They laughed at that, patted her hands. "If you have daughters, you'll see, they choose their own paths, however treacherous. You can only watch, or they will run, perhaps slip and fall."

She'd glimpsed the American boys on their yacht this morning – tall, tanned and seeming years older than the island girls they ushered aboard. As Bianca accepted her place in the arms of the tallest at the bow, Patrizia had hesitated, turned, and on seeing her mother at the quay, waved. Then she too stepped on board.

Julia isn't sure why it bothered her so. Perhaps because Bianca, for all her leggy Italian beauty, reminds her of herself at that age. Perhaps because she recalls the thrill of giving up life in Britain to marry a man twice her age and move to a lake island where people believe an abundance of paper flowers will keep their families from harm.

As their girls grew older, Julia told Francesco her wish to relocate them to England, give them the chance to know her parents better, experience city living.

He'd scoffed at the suggestion. "Where better to be young than here?" He spread his arms wide to encompass the entirety of Monte Isola, Lake Iseo and the Italian sky overhead. It was difficult to argue on days when the sky shone pure blue above the houses and the subtle aroma of ripening limes competed only with the scent of roasting fish.

Besides, as he pointed out, what would he do in rainy Britain?

When he died, stripped from his family by a latent heart defect, Julia's sister came to the funeral. At the graveside, she'd murmured: "Now you can come home."

Yet somehow his death secured Julia in place, as though staying on Monte Isola had been his dying wish. She could never leave now.

But her daughters could. They are beholden to no one. She thinks of them now, on the boat of the American boys, and imagines them laughing as they plot their escapes. She clings to the fact that they're sailing on a lake, with no access to the sea.

Towards the end of the afternoon she helps Chiara tidy up; markers re-capped, paper tendrils swept away.

Matteo is at the waterfront tying up his naèt – the flat-bottomed fishing boat his half sisters would have spurned. Beyond him, cypress trees stand up to their knobbly knees in the unruffled water.

"I saw the girls, Julia," he greets her, "with a load of *asini*." He brays loudly, reminding her *asini* is the word for donkeys.

She smiles with him, but he must notice the concern in her eyes. "Want I should go get them?" He puffs up his chest in bravado.

"No, but thanks, I'm just being silly," she tells him. "Bianca would be so embarrassed!"

"Bianca will be embarrassed whatever you do." He shrugs and laughs. He married three years ago, has a son tiny enough to hold in his arms. Julia envies him that.

At his invitation she joins his young family at a bar overlooking the water. Heat rises from the stone of the buildings; lizards skittering into the tiny cracks that flowers cleave to, vibrant pink against the mortar. Francesco would have known their names, in Italian if not English. She touches the petals with a fingertip, working out the teardrop cuts needed to recreate them in crepe.

They order the caffè ristretto Julia has learnt to love. Matteo's wife Alessia offers her the baby and she takes solace in his warm weight, the softness of his skin against her lips. She turns him towards the lake, points out the storks billowing by overhead, the ducks busy below. In the distance, the little private islands are hazy, their rich-man follies indistinct.

A sleek boat is heading towards Carzano at speed. Julia stands as she recognises it as the one her girls boarded this morning. "Look, your aunts are on that!" she tells the child, who blinks, no more curious about this than he is about the wind shifting through poppies' bright faces.

Matteo stands too, but suddenly, with an urgency that catches at her edges. The wind shudders across the limpid water and she hears voices shrilling from the boat like distress calls.

"Take your son," she says to Alessia, thrusting the baby towards her. She hurries after Matteo down to the quayside, where two of the boys are making a hash of bringing the boat in. They seem younger now, closer to Bianca's age than Julia guessed.

At first she can't see the girls, then she spies Patrizia crouching at the bow, the fingers of one hand crammed into her mouth as she used to when she was little. Bianca is there too, sitting down. She's cradling the head and torso of the tallest American in her lap.

"What happened?" Julia hears herself shriek. She can see blood on Bianca's arms. "Bianca, what happened?"

"Mama!" she cries, and sounds anxious in a way that grips Julia's heart.

Matteo assists the lads in tying up, then he's aboard. Julia watches him bend to look into Patrizia's face, check she's ok, before going to her sister. She tells him something quick and garbled, and Julia sees his expression go through concern, annoyance, resignation.

"He'll be fine," he tells her. "Stupid *asino*."

"Matteo?" Julia cries.

"The blood isn't Bianca's," he assures her, and she feels her heart relax a notch. "The Americans swam ashore to one of the islands."

"We told them not to," Patrizia puts in, "but they wouldn't listen!"

My good, clever girl, Julia mouths to herself.

"You know how these people are," Matteo says. "No unexpected visitors tolerated. There were guard dogs. The boy has been well chewed, no more."

Matteo helps the boy to stand and he limps ashore. Julia wonder if his friends should have taken him to the mainland hospital, but beneath the sheen of blood the wounds don't look so bad.

"Hope your inoculations are up to date," she comments. The boy looks at her askance, pale beneath his tan, and she waits for the familiar surprised "You're English?" but it doesn't come.

Matteo takes the Americans to find the island's doctor. Patrizia and Bianca lean into Julia, one on each side. She holds their warm, lithe bodies in her arms, wanting to keep them there, keep them safe. "You're ok?" she asks them, but they're already wriggling away.

"Fine, Mama!" they cry, heedless of her concern. She watches the pair run off together along the island paths; keeps her eyes on them until they disappear from view.

Strawberry Thief

THE HIDE IS empty but for herself and Jonathan. In the clearing beyond the structure, birds cavort – more species than she can name. Jonathan would know them all. He understood their code of feathers and colours in a way she's never been able to grasp.

She reaches into the bag beside her and draws the thermos out. The cup that sits neatly over its lid makes her pause, flooded with a memory. At the hospice, she'd crushed strawberries against its rim, fed the crimson pulp into his mouth with a teaspoon. He'd swallowed, then muttered, soft enough that she had to lean close: "Wrong season for strawbs. Where'd you get 'em?"

Not wanting to name the shop she'd bought them from, where they nestled in the fridge alongside own-brand sausage rolls, she smiled back and said: "The pick-your-own. Remember?"

That lie had seemed worth it for the brief lessening of the pain she saw in his mud-brown eyes. She popped one of the berries into her own mouth, chewing fast. It was cold against her tongue, and lacked the burst of sweetness she craved, but its flavour connected her to the moment, to him.

"Tell me a secret," she asked, and he blinked, thoughtful.

"When I go…," he began, and her hands tightened around his, "I hope I get to fly."

That was the last thing he said to her.

The first time they'd met at the pick-your-own, they'd been small enough that she could get lost among the raspberry canes, emerging into the field of crouch-high bushes glistening with crimson fruit. She'd crammed them in by the handful, juice spilling from her lips, listening to the humming of bees and the distant chatter of families, until a boy stepped towards her. He eyed her reddened hands and mouth, then leaned in and told her a secret.

Each summer he had a new one to tell, his breath tickling in her ear. "All strawbs used to be white," he told her one year, "They blush because of what they saw."

"What'd they see?" she asked, and he led her deep into the loganberry canes, unfastened his shorts and stood with a serene smile as she examined with intrigue the rosy heat that climbed from his groin.

Before long they took to meeting in the woodland, lying together in the shade of a clutch of ash trees as he named the birds they could see darting. "Chaffinch, song thrush, goldfinch, blue tit, jackdaw." The jackdaw was so lumbering compared with the others – dark and greedy beneath its cap of grey. "He's the smartest of the lot," Jonathan insisted, "He's the one that can figure out puzzles, will pick out shiny things."

"Like what?"

"Jewellery," he said. "Gems."

"What use are gems to a bird?" she'd asked, and he laughed.

"Catches their eye 'cause it looks like water, then they're curious so they take it home."

Later years had brought other discoveries, one resulting in the start of their eldest daughter and an end to their pick-your-own visits.

Thinking of that draws up the memory of a time soon after when he leaned in close, whispering in her ear: "You're the jewel in my eye."

The engagement ring he gave her boasted an aquamarine like a piece of water and two small diamonds that danced with light.

She was the thief – that was his first secret to her, the day he stepped out of the shadows and whispered in her ear. The strawberries she was gobbling ought to have been paid for. "If they'd weighed you on the way in, then on the way out, maybe they could do it, but for now you better go and wash yourself. Scrub the evidence away."

"How d'you know to do that?" she asked, and he grinned.

"Because I done it too." And he lifted one red-stained finger to his lips, making her laugh.

Now, at the hide in the woodland he'd loved, she opens the flask. It's full of him, of his ashes, mixed liberally with nuts, seeds, and oats. She steps outside and watches the birds retreat, then layers him over the frosted ground. Once she's tucked back out of sight, the thrushes and wrens return. They're fastidious, she can see that, picking out the grains they want from the dust he once was. A few bits must go with them, though. And if one crumb of ash ends up in a gullet he'll get what he asked for. He'll get to fly.

Her engagement ring glints where it fell with the ash and seeds, catching the early spring sunshine. A jackdaw hops down, eyes bright as mud, stabs out with its beak and flutters away.

She sits there a while longer, watching shadows move through the trees, murmuring secrets to the wind.

Part Two

Light

The Moth Room

H E FOLLOWS HER home from the ball, trailing in the pitch of her laughter. She's taken off her shoes for dancing and runs barefoot through the ragged streets, giggles glinting in her wake.

The warehouse she leads him to is shuttered into rooms, each with its own door to unlock. Hers is labelled The Moth Room. When he asks why, she stands on tiptoe and draws down a narrow box. "They're in here," she breathes. "Unless these are the wasp carapaces I collect." She fires a glance at him; he flinches as he spies the sting in her eyes. "No, I'm sure of it, this is the moths."

At her bidding, he peels off the lid, reveals layer upon layer of little furry stiffs — some brittle and brown as rolled-up autumn leaves, others banded with scarlet.

"Where are their wings?" he gasps.

And laughing, she spins, showing off the rustle and flutter of her nip-waisted gown.

Far From the Farm

I F EILIDH LEANS close to the bedroom window and breathes out, she can make the world beyond grow cold and fog-filled. She dapples her fingertips against the glass, creating pools of light that shine sharp and ice-bright. The sky is yellow today, swollen with clouds heavy with something chillier than rain.

It won't snow here. This southern city would grind to a halt if a few sparse flakes fell from the sky.

That's what Franny says, anyways. It bothers Eilidh to think of her old gran managing the farm alone, without anyone to ride the tractor with. Who'll bound out to drag the gate open, close it again once she's through? Worry makes Eilidh's chest tighten, forces her to grip the windowsill till her fingertips whiten.

She breathes in, breathes out, pictures the hills of Skye glowing purple and orange where heather and gorse have taken hold.

In the city where she and Mam now live, hills are lined with shops and crowded with shoppers, regardless of the time of day. Paths wind sedately through parks, snaking into roads where people rush on foot, by bike, in car or bus; dashing to wherever they need to go. Here, even free time seems frantic.

Her mam has a job at the university, helping foreign students who look as lost as Eilidh feels. Each day she sets off early, trusting Eilidh to leave as the clock ticks towards the school bell's trill. The school itself is tall and grey, filled with teenagers who gawp whenever Eilidh dares speak. Increasingly she stays silent, gazing through the classroom window and daydreaming about the farm and the life she's left behind. Sometimes she's so absorbed by this that the teacher has to shout her name, making the others snigger. "Eyelid, oi, Eyelid! Teach wants ya!" Her cheeks burn as she stumbles over the reply to whatever question has been thrust her way.

Lunchtimes are spent huddled in the shadows cast by the science block, trying to ignore the hooked glances and gibes that filter her way across the yard.

The one class she enjoys is art, when they get to prop up easels, blend hues, and pour onto pages whatever fills their minds. Eilidh paints glowing green and indigo hillsides, and, just for the hell of it, here and there, a smattering of white blobby sheep with their wee black faces. She knows her paintings are childish in the eyes of the other kids, who are busy creating surrealist ink drawings of iguana-headed girls and botanically accurate studies of exotic flora. The art teacher, who is possibly older than Franny and a whole lot woollier round the edges, is too busy looking forward to the end of term to be bothered.

The boy who sits next to her in art class comes over and takes a look sometimes, standing behind her and staring into her painting as though through a window. She doesn't mind. He's another quiet one like her, cannie and self-contained. Occasionally he'll point to some detail, a particular cloud or a wedge of stone on the painted hillside, and murmur: "Nice." She wonders what it is about those particular sections that attract him, but returns his smile and carries on. His voice soothes her somehow, just as Franny used to be able to calm her out of nightmares and tantrums and the fright of storms, reshaping fear to comfort with a few words ("hear the thunder? That's giants grumbling their promise to keep us safe."). His presence slows her heartbeat until peace steals over her and she finds herself beaming at him from under her fringe.

She asked Franny to text before they packed up the car and left, but Franny refused. "My mobile's for emergencies only, my wee sunshine. Besides, can you imagine these stubby farmer's fingers tapping out messages on those toty buttons?"

Eilidh can, as it happens, because she's watched her gran's deftness when knitting, and her firm gentleness with chittering ewes tangled to barbed wire fences, her fingers' strength when working the animals loose. It's a sight that's awed Eilidh more than once, seeing the sheep's yellow eyes grow tranquil until the barbs are eased away and the creature can skitter off to join its flock.

"No, I'll send you postcards," Franny declared, seeming pleased with the idea. "So many postcards your walls'll be full."

They've been in Bristol a couple of months and it's already almost true, each one marked with just a sentence or two of Franny's scratchy, barely decipherable words; a code for Eilidh to make sense of, that no one else will understand.

On her most recent postcard – now stuck to the back of the bedroom door – Franny's scrawl reports that it's already white in the valleys – snow blooming like mushrooms in crevices of trees. Eilidh can hear the creak of the snow underfoot, pictures the sheep exhaling mist against the glittering air. Most of them will be pregnant by now, ready to lamb next year. She wonders if any will come over Christmas when she and Mam are home. The stretch of time between now and then seems endless.

Eilidh closes her eyes, tries to imagine what her gran's doing right now. If it's bitter out, she might be somewhere sheltered, dyeing yarn sheared from the sheep in summer. Yarn dyeing is always one of Eilidh's best jobs to help with. She loves gathering the ingredients, mixing them in a pot over the fire, secretly pretending she and Franny are a pair of witches, although she knows she's too old for such games. The earthy aromas swirled out to fill the barn: the rich sweet smell of simmering berries, or the dankness of horseshoe fungus. The best bit is seeing the colour take, changing the yarn from cream to pink or purple, or a myriad shades of grey and brown. Most of the hues come from plants they've foraged: bog myrtle, bracken, birch bark, nettles, heather tops, and tree beards – the grey lichen that grows over branches and trunks, dripping down like cloudy water.

Eilidh blinks her eyes open. Overhead there's a flurry of footsteps, and a door slams in one of the nearby flats. If she doesn't get a wriggle on she'll be late enough to be put on warning. Worse, Mam might get called in and given a stern talking to by a teacher with half her qualifications and experience. Then Eilidh'll have to endure the anxious looks, the half-smiles and tentative tiptoed investigations into her wellbeing, just as happened after Da left them way back when. The trick is to turn up moments late instead of minutes, pay the least possible amount of attention while there.

Eilidh unfurls reluctantly, stamps her feet against the floor half to get the blood back into them, half to say a sort of hello to the people who live downstairs. She slings her school bag over one shoulder, runs down the staircase to the ground floor stomping with enough force to make her teeth shake in her head. The effort cheers her up, somehow.

A voice calls out as she nears the entrance foyer, bumping into her thoughts. It's the postie, a grin glimmering out. "Morning Eilidh." He's the only person in this place who says her name right, pronouncing it Ay-lee, not Eyelid.

Postie always makes a joke of the postcards he delivers, claiming to have read all kinds of mushy messages from some boyfriend he's dreamt up for her. "Says he misses you, he does, says his heart is smashed to bits" or, occasionally, as he hands her the card: "Mind your mum don't see this one, ai. Enough to blush a penguin pink!" Which, naturally, makes Eilidh turn crimson and snatch it from him, even though she knows it's from Franny and is probably about foraging through hedgerows.

The postie is another newcomer to the city, his accent lilting in a way the local voices lack. He seems at home here – comfortable in his skin in a way Eilidh hasn't felt since surrounded by Skye's fields and clouds.

Today he has a parcel in his hands. "Here you go, love. Birthday, is it?"

She shakes her head as she accepts it from him, seeing the scrawl of Franny's handwriting on the top. The package has almost no weight at all.

He takes his time as he stuffs letters into each of the different flats' post boxes, humming softly to himself. Eilidh hesitates then sits on the bottom step of the stairs, wrestling the tape from the brown paper.

The contents slither onto her lap: gold and mustard, scented with lanolin and hilltop air. A scarf knitted by Franny.

Postie whistles low and approving. "Nice."

Eilidh returns his smile, draping the soft fragrant wool around her. The farm suddenly doesn't seem so far away. She breathes in deep, stands up and steps out of the building, ready to face the walk to school.

Traffic rumbles as it eases through the narrow spaces, reminding her of Franny's story of giants growling their promises to keep her safe. Far overhead the yellow clouds hang, heavy with something too cold to fall.

Breaking Up With You Burns Like Fire

THEY DRESSED IN the dark, fumbling over bootlaces and coal-black buttons. Lucinda picked up the ceramic gargoyle Crispin had given her early in their romance. He chose the straw doll Lucinda wove for their first anniversary.

It felt right to leave the offerings in the coppice outside the house they'd shared.

Lucinda deposited the gargoyle in an ivy-looped tree near the entrance. Crispin propped the doll against the exit stile.

Later, witnesses claimed the fire flared up at opposite ends of the woodland – two blazes rushing inwards till they fell into an embrace that lit up the sky.

Flamingos and Ham

I WAS TWELVE when the ruling came in, banning certain words, colours, and clothing. It seemed farcical at first. My mum and dad laughed in disbelief as they watched the news.

"How can they outlaw pink?" Dad hooted. "What about flamingos and… and, ham?!"

Mum grimaced, clutching her crochet hook. "Why forbid hats, and yarn? What are they afraid of?"

Neither mentioned the words considered inflammatory. I think they understood even then that to utter them aloud could be dangerous.

At school the next day new uniforms were distributed. The boiler suits came in pewter-grey or beige. We giggled as we slipped them on over our regular clothes, teasing each other that we resembled an army. Suki was the only one unsmiling. "We look like clones," she said. "No boys, no girls, no personalities."

"What are they afraid of?" I agreed, speaking the words softly – already wary of being overheard.

No one knew who might be listening, ready to share transgressions. Some instinct was taking hold; making us discreet.

On the first day of winter I saw the man who ran the art shop arrested for wearing a knitted cap. He was seething in his handcuffs, snarling about infringements of human rights. I jolted to hear the prohibited words ring through the icy air.

His eyes met mine as they jostled him into a van. "Don't forget," he said, "Don't let them make you believe this is normal. You wore pink once, and ran for the hell of it. Don't forget those…"

The door slid shut and he was gone. I watched the van disappear around a slippery corner and tried to remember the differences between then and now. It felt a lifetime ago.

Lamp Black

Two children on the other side of the station are playing close to the platform edge. One is giving the other a piggyback ride, stepping along the yellow warning line like it's a tightrope. None of the adults within reach intervenes.

I think about shouting out, but don't want to startle her. As I watch, she wobbles and staggers towards the train tracks. My hands clench and unclench at my waist.

She drops the child she's carrying.

The smaller one lands on one foot, flailing for a moment, bunches quivering. She catches her balance, pulling herself upright. The locomotive roars up behind them and they disappear from my view.

"Train's here!" I imagine their excitement – no thought for the danger they were in seconds before.

The train storms out of the station, sweeping the children with it.

I leave too, walking briskly back to my terraced house where I can close the door behind me and shut out the world.

The relief sings through me. Leaning against the hallway wall, I drag in air like someone almost drowned.

In the kitchen I set out my things and paint and paint until the sun shifts down the sky. One after another, I scratch out wild, windswept scenes in raw umber, lamp black and grey; creaking tree branches; fierce, fragmented light. In the lower half of the canvas I add railway tracks and the distant sliver of an approaching train. I hum as I work, filling the silence with the soft sound of my own buzzing breath.

Lamp black always used to seem like a trick to me. Like the kind of thing Dan would say to catch me out. *Sure, rivers are full of shopping trolleys because water acts like a magnet – that's how the tides work.* Then he'd laugh along with everyone else when I believed him simply because I couldn't see why he'd bother to lie.

For ages after Dan I regarded lamp black paint with suspicion. Surely lamps are bright things – light, not dark?

Then a man in the art shop mentioned it was named for the lamp soot it was made from. Discovering that felt like unknotting a mystery. I held the knowledge smugly to me. Part of me wants someone to ask me about it, so I can explain and show that I'm in on it too.

But who could ask me when I keep myself so separate?

The front door crashes closed, shaking the house and scattering my focus. I glance at the clock. Somehow it's after six already.

I've done nothing about tea.

"We're home, Mum!" Mira cries. I picture her and the little one, Jenna, sniffing the air, searching for clues that I've forgotten to cook for them.

"Good, I missed you," I fib, wiping my hands on a rag. For good measure I add: "I missed you both! If you're hungry, we can order pizza. What'd you say?"

Jenna sidles in, eyes flickering round the room like she's checking for things that might attack. "I like pizza," she announces, as though I might not know.

I think about telling her I saw them on the platform almost tumbling in front of the train, do a sharp scold like parents are supposed to.

But that would give away that I was there.

To hide my uncertainty, I sit down, hands pressed flat beneath my legs. At once she scrambles onto my lap.

I pull my hands free and hug her awkwardly, wondering what it is that makes her do that kind of thing. Her hair in its lopsided bunches smells faintly unclean.

"After tea you need to have a bath and wash your hair," I tell her. "You can do that by yourself, can't you? Big girl like you?"

She looks unsure, but doesn't disagree.

"Mira, order the pizza and get them to deliver it, yeah? Menu's by the phone." I'm still clutching the little one, reluctant for some reason to let go.

"What's the clues for tomorrow," Jenna asks, and I release my grip on her.

I'm tired of coming up with clues each night. The alternative is having them here all day, which would be so much worse.

Sometimes I think about being the one to leave, just walking out and letting them fend for themselves. But this is my home, my refuge. I was here first.

"Wait till Mira joins us," I say to buy myself some time. She slides off my lap, leaving a cold spot on my thighs where her warmth has been.

While we wait for the pizza I tidy my art things and think hard. It's increasingly difficult to come up with places to send them. Five days to go, I remind myself. In five days, school will start again, we'll slip back into our usual, simpler existence and I won't have to wrack my brain finding ways to get them out of the house each morning.

This morning's first clue was: "Your father loves water."

Mira exclaimed: "The seaside!" Sometimes I think she misunderstands on purpose.

Second clue: "Your father loves yellow ducks."

Jenna guessed: "The wildfowl park?"

How could they be so dim? *Must take after you*, Dan muttered in my head.

Panicked, I blurted: "Your father loves flannels", which confused them, until Mira lit up.

"Bathtime! Daddy's in Bath!"

Thank Christ for that.

They've been playing the "Where's Daddy Now?" game all summer, setting out daily in search of a man who's been absent for most of their lives.

Mira chews the last slice of pizza and gets the light in her eyes that tells me I must be ready. "Where's Daddy now?" she asks. "He wasn't in Bath. We just found loads of tourists and, whatdyacallem? Busters?"

"Buskers," I correct. "Ok, here's the first clue. Your father loves spires."

"What's spires?" Jenna asks.

"They're the pointy things on top of churches, silly. Everyone knows that," Mira scoffs, then frowns. "That's right, isn't it, Mummy?"

"Yes." I nod. "They're on top of cathedrals too, so keep that in mind."

"Next clue!"

"Your father loves great big drinks."

They exchange glances. Have I made it too difficult?

"Final clue," I say. "Your father loves places that the sun can't reach."

They still look blank. The smile I've glued on falters. I wonder what to do.

Then Mira whispers in Jenna's ear, and Jenna goes: "Ooooh", so that's all right.

After they go to bed, I make peanut butter sandwiches for them to take on their adventure. I listen to the sound of trains swooshing by in the darkness and allow myself a glow of pride. How many six- and eight-year-olds could figure out those clues mean the city of Wells?

The next day, I give Mira cash for their bus fares, and close the door behind them.

I get out my things and begin to put the finishing touches to my painting of a wide-open sky with lamp black rain clouds glooming on the horizon.

By mid-afternoon, I've finished. I pack away my things, washing the brushes·and palette with care in the kitchen sink. The picture I leave propped drying against a cupboard door. It's been a good day.

I nip down to the corner shop and buy the ingredients for a shepherd's pie. I'm pretty sure that's Mira's favourite. Jenna tends to follow Mira's lead in everything, so that should be ok.

When six o'clock ticks round, the dinner's ready. I'd award myself a moment of self-satisfaction, but for the fact they're still not home.

They've never been late before.

I take my time laying the table, trying not to let the jagged sensation in my veins take hold. I set out three tumblers, cutlery, a trio of plates.

My movements grow visibly jerkier.

I pour fruit juice into a jug, overfilling it. Sunset-tinted water splashes onto the floor and I have to wipe it up. That takes a while, but when I straighten up, sparks flashing at the corners of my eyes, I'm still alone.

The pie's lid of mashed potato is looking frazzled. I take it from the oven and place it squarely in the middle of the table. I'm sharply aware that I haven't put it on a mat. Perhaps it will make a big black mark on the wood that I can blame the girls for and shout at them about.

It's almost half past six.

I take off the oven glove and chuck it on the countertop, then very deliberately reach my finger towards the dish the pie is bubbling in. Anger snickers through me – the sound of a train flying over tracks – and I push my fingertip against the hot Pyrex. It's just for a second, but pain shoots into my head like a light clicking on.

I whip my hand from the dish; see the fleshy ball of red on the tip turning ice-white.

The front door creaks open, slams shut, and I hear their chatter explode into the house. Their voices sound even higher pitched than usual.

Mira rushes in first, ablaze with excitement. "Mum! We found him!"

I hold my throbbing finger to my side. "Your dinner's getting cold. Sit down."

She barely seems to hear me, hopping up and down like she's suddenly younger than the little one, who's still lurking in the doorway.

I glower at the pair of them. "*Sit down!*"

My voice cuts through Mira's unfathomable joy and she seems to shrink inside her clothes. I watch as she takes her place at the table, feet scuffing the floor in her hurry.

"You too," I say to the other one, more gently. "Sorry I snapped. I was…" I pause, pressing my palms to my waist, blinking. "I was worried about you both. You're late." Something Mira said as she bounced in nags at me. I sit at the narrow end of the table between them. "Why *are* you late?"

Mira raises her face, and a smile leaks out. "We found him, Mummy," she whispers. "He was where you said. At the Cathedral."

"What?" I ladle portions of shepherd's pie onto plates and push one in front of her.

"We figured out the clues." She counts off on her fingers: "Spires, drinks, no sunshine… You meant that pub down near the shopping centre, didn't you? The one called the Cathedral!" She jiggles on her chair, beaming. "We waited till it opened, walked right in. The barman tried to make us leave, but I told him we were after our dad."

I stare at her, and at Jenna, who avoids my eyes and jabs her fork into the pie, running the tines through singed mashed potato like she's digging up a field.

My throat seems full, though I haven't put anything in my mouth yet. I put down my cutlery with a clatter and hear myself cough.

"He sold us a packet of crisps to share and we waited all morning, but then this man came in and I just knew it! We knew, didn't we, Jenna?"

"What d'you mean, you knew?" I ask, trying to ignore the rushing in my ears. I keep seeing the painting in the corner of my vision: trees thrashing in the turmoil of a rising wind. I picture a branch tearing loose, plunging onto the railway tracks; passengers ignorant in their carriages – no idea what's about to rip through their lives.

"That he's our dad!" Mira says. "The barman, he told the man that we were looking for our dad, and I said I hadn't seen him since I was three, so he might not know me. The man, Mum, he stared at me and said, 'I know you all right, sweetie.' He called me sweetie, Mum!"

"This man…" There are bodies strewn over the tracks: broken

bodies and twisted metal. "This man told you he's your father?"

Jenna glances at me quickly, but Mira is still grinning. "Tomorrow we're going to meet him at the pub and then go to his house so we can get to know him better. Isn't it amazing?"

"Amazing," I agree, wondering what the hell to do.

I don't sleep that night, just pace the house listening to the distant sound of trains. I look in at the girls' bedroom whenever I pass it. Each time I do, Jenna stares right back at me, eyes huge in the pink glow of the night-light.

When morning comes, I watch them leave the house. I get out my things, squeezing watercolours out of their tubes onto a saucer: cobalt blue crimson leaf green cadium yellow lamp black.

The roaring in my ears is louder than ever. I take my fattest brush and smear it across the saucer through the colours, and cast it down. It clatters from the saucer to the floor, showering a dismal multi-hued rainbow across the kitchen.

My head is full of twisted metal.

The slam of the front door echoes behind me. I don't stop running till the shopping mall is in my sights, looming over the Cathedral pub.

Halting just outside, I drag in air. Then I wrench open the door and march in.

My eyes take a moment to adjust to the lamp black shadows of the inside. At first it seems to be entirely empty; my heart flutters frantically until I hear the voice of my eldest daughter. It's piping from one of the high-backed booths.

I stride to the booth, hanging onto the anger that's keeping me upright, and see my daughters sitting with a lank-haired stranger. His red-rimmed eyes are roaming over Mira like he's deciding whether he's hungry enough to eat her.

"What the hell d'you think you're doing with these girls?" I demand as loudly as I can manage. All three of them jump.

Mira looks from me to the man, the man to me.

Relief pinches pink circles onto Jenna's cheeks.

The man glares at me, but his eyes have gone shifty. "What's it to you?"

"Mira, Jenna, I don't care what he's told you, but this man is not your father," I bark.

A shock of confusion sweeps across Mira, turning to a sudden stomach-churning alarm.

I reach out my hands.

My girls slide out of the booth and in an instant I've got one gripping tight on either side of me. I glare triumphantly at the stranger. "I've phoned the police and told them what you're up to, you sicko," I tell him.

He leans back in his seat, leering at me with something like contempt. "Know what, lass? Takes one to know one."

I shake my head and turn heel, leading my children out of the sour-smelling pub and into the sun-filled streets.

It's only when we walk into our terraced house and close the door behind us, shutting out the world, that I let go of their hands. I kneel down and open my arms.

It's a surprise, but Jenna's the one who comes to me first, something like forgiveness, hot in her small body. I grip her tight in the crook of one elbow, and I keep the other arm outstretched.

Elevated Truths

"THE ELEVATOR WAS invented by a woman in 1852," I tell my father when he looks up from the article he's writing and asks me what I've learnt today. "Her name was Elisha Graves Otis, and she founded the Otis Elevator Company. See, women can do anything men can."

He looks at me over his laptop screen, his eyebrows doing that weird pinch in, thrust out move that means he's not sure what to correct you on first.

"That's not quite right," he says, and I scowl. "A version of the *elevator*, as you call it, was invented more than a thousand years before that, by a man named Archimedes." He grabs one of my braids and tugs it lightly. "And we know it as a lift, dear. You've been watching too much American telly."

I'm scowling so hard my lips are quivering.

Mum pinches him on the arm. "Apologise to your daughter for upsetting her," she hisses. I've heard them argue about this before – she tells him everyone deserves to feel like a hero occasionally. He believes truth is better, fairer, even to an eight-year-old like me.

He snorts, and Mum glares at him.

"Sorry to upset you, love," he says, "I'm trying to equip you to deal with the world. We can't always be right, can we?"

I wonder if he's using the type of 'we' that only refers to me.

I want to prove him wrong, so after tea I go online and check Wikipedia. It doesn't mention the Archimedes bloke Dad was on about, but it does reveal something far worse. If facial hair is to be believed, Elisha Graves Otis was a man.

My heart breaks, just a little.

I look at the photo, and I make a decision, choosing what angle to take on the story I plan to share.

Dad's in the living room, re-reading his column.

"Dad, Elisha Graves Otis may not have invented the elevator, but she did invent a special safety brake that stops people dying in them, which is at least as important," I declare. I turn around, preparing to storm from the room after my final delivery. "And she could grow an amazing beard and moustache! Women can do anything."

2004 <> 1914

After being made redundant from the paper, Dad stops correcting me on every little thing. I find I miss his pickiness. He says he's freelance now, which seems to mean he does a lot of writing for free. He calls this writing 'on spec.'

I stomp downstairs on a weekday morning and find him sitting at the kitchen table, laptop open.

"Did you know that the First World War began because the band Franz Ferdinand insulted some Austrian duke in 1914?" I ask, mangling the truth so badly I'm sure he won't be able to resist feeding me the facts. I pour cereal into a bowl and contemplate it before adding milk. "And TV serials are named that because the episodes cram together like cornflakes in a bowl."

He raises his eyebrows briefly. "Is that so?"

I stare at him, a shiver going through me so that milk sloshes onto the countertop.

"Careful!" he says, but his tone is distracted. I think about spilling some milk closer to him, maybe splashing his keyboard a bit.

Mum comes in, wearing a smile-lie to hide her concern. "All right, love?" She runs one hand down Dad's cheek where his sideburns are turning grey. "Busy day planned?"

"Mmm," he says, "Very. Beth's coming over. We're going to work on that feature pitch." His eyebrows pinch out and down. I don't know how to read that expression.

Beth got made redundant in the same wave of cuts as Dad. She saunters into our kitchen with her hair trailing and bracelets clacking. Her breath is cherry cough syrup. Leaning so close to Dad that her breasts are almost in his face, she scans the pitch Dad has drafted and trills that he's her hero.

I see Mum's mouth purse over her cup of coffee and wonder if she remembers her line about us all needing to feel like heroes, if only for a moment. I wonder if she was using the type of 'we' that only referred to me.

2006 <> 1989

After school I catch a bus to Dad and Beth's flat. They're on the 8th floor of their building. The elevator is an ancient metal cylinder that Beth has nicknamed 'the beast'. If she's with me when the doors slide closed, she does a little squeak and pretends we've been eaten. I smile-lie and bite back the urge to remind her I'm fourteen, not four.

I prefer to ride the elevator alone and think of Elisha Graves Otis. In my head, I paint her with the beard in the Wikipedia photo, but she's very much the woman I first imagined her as. I envision her running her company, standing at the head of a boardroom instructing her engineers on how they're going to create the device she's designed.

The elevator doors ping open.

"It's me!" I yell as I let myself into the flat. I go straight into the kitchen and open the fridge door, blocking my view to the living room. That way Dad will have time to get from couch to bedroom and pull on proper clothes if he's still in his pajamas.

There are cherry tomatoes wizening in the salad drawer, and a Peach Melba yogurt one day past its sell-by-date. I grab it.

"Hello, love." Dad sidles into the room.

'How's the writing going?" I ask, spooning a small orange mountain into my mouth.

"Oh, great, making real progress." Dad's eyebrows pinch outwards and down.

I used to think that movement showed he was lying, but I've

come to understand it means he's trying to convince himself that what he's saying is true. A subtle difference.

"How's school? What did you learn today?" he asks.

I think for a moment. "That the Berlin Wall fell in November 1989 because of an unexpectedly mild autumn. The wall defrosted and all the bricks melted."

He laughs. "End of the Cold War, eh? Clever girl. Gonna to ace those history exams!"

"In a couple of years, yeah."

He doesn't seem to mind my correction.

He looks tired, I think. His grey hair is thinning; I can see his scalp shining through. Mum would have told him it looks distinguished – one of her elevated truths. I wonder if he misses living with us.

I'm still thinking about that when I step into the elevator and press the G that will deposit me at ground level. I watch each floor pass by. Seven, six, five...

On impulse I hit the emergency stop button, sending a silent prayer up to the ghost of Elisha Graves Otis.

She works her magic. The elevator jolts and sways, but slides safely to a halt. It dangles in the lift shaft, awaiting my next instruction.

I type into my phone quickly. "Dad! Stuck in lift! Help!!"

I press send and picture the text message zinging in: Dad scanning the screen and jolting upright with urgency. Rushing to save me, his only daughter. Being my hero.

Not Every Wound Can Heal

A DARK ARTEFACT hangs from the ceiling of the Baroque church. It resembles a bit of branch, or a stick covered in rags. Our tour guide tells us it's a mummified arm.

Afterwards Tim and I each remember the story differently. He's convinced it's the relic of a saint. I'm sure it's the limb of a thief who tried to steal jewels from a statue of the Virgin Mary, and that she came to life and twisted his arm entirely off.

Perhaps it's not an arm at all.

I can't get it out of my head.

I think about it as I stand in the shower soaping my own limbs. The scar from the break just above my right elbow glows white in the morning sun.

As we walk in the street, I eye the shadow of my swinging arm and imagine it dangling, stinking, rotting, from the ceiling of a church.

In the evening, I order a plate of ribs, but find the meat glues to my teeth. It feels like I'm eating a corpse.

I suppose I actually am.

Tim tells me to stop being so stupid. He tells me to think of something else.

Like what? I ask.

Think about us, he says. Think about me.

I think about us, and wonder if he's really the saint his mother claims he is for taking me back after I ran away.

I think about him, and wonder whether he'd steal jewels as a romantic gesture to demonstrate his love for me.

I wonder if the next time he decides I've done something wrong he'll twist my arm entirely off.

That night I look at him lying in bed beside me, lit by the moon slipping into our hotel room, and I see how the hair on his slack arm spells out each of my mistakes.

I imagine his arm hanging from the narthex of the church, far out of reach, withered and pathetic.

Somewhere nearby a bell tolls the hour.

Little Blessings

MY COUNSELLOR ONCE told me to count my blessings, so I do.

I have my work. That's a blessing. When the alarm clock shocks me out of sleep to the bleakest, rainiest mornings, it gives me a reason to uncurl myself, step outside, present my best side to the world.

I have my health. That's a blessing. It equips me for the long, tedious walk to the train station. When my umbrella crumples, defeated, I stride onwards, strong.

And in its own way, the commute is a blessing too – a chance to travel faster than I can run without any discernible effort, an opportunity to people-watch, nose into the exterior layer of lives that are none of my business. A blessing of sorts even on a particularly frantic morning, when the trains are delayed and everyone is single-minded with one intent: get to work, and a man shoves me out of his way with such unexpected force I topple against the train that's waiting. At least it wasn't the moment before the locomotive arrived, at least I didn't plummet down the chasm of the tracks, get gulped down by the train as it arrived. And to add to the celebratory sense of survival, success, at boarding the train in one complete piece, I have that odd, self-righteous enjoyment of being the wronged, of hearing other commuters berate my reckless shover. Of imagining his shame, quietly revelling in it till I almost feel I ought to apologise to him.

Almost, but not quite.

I know I haven't mentioned any of the things most normal people would expect: family, friends, all that bumf. I haven't included my husband. Or my son. Perhaps that's the one that secretly bothers me, the fact I have omitted my son.

He, my son, the boy, got in touch recently. Inexplicably adult and grown, able to write, work a computer. Track me down.

Last time I saw him he was barely three. Now he's thirty. A grown man claiming to be my little boy.

I deleted the first email, so sure was I that it was spam. But I couldn't sleep afterwards, just lay in the darkness, thinking – who would know to try to con me in this way? Barely anyone knows the boy ever existed, not even my husband.

And the details in the second, persistent email were unnervingly accurate. "You used to call me Boy," he types. "I know my registered name was Adrian. My adoptive parents named me Peter."

The ultimate Lost Boy, found.

And then he mentioned a train journey we'd taken together once, how the woman on the next seat along had a box full of squirming white mice she'd let him peek in at.

I recall those mice too, and that journey. We were travelling to the town I grew up in, on the Hampshire coast, to see the boy's grandparents. I tried to sidle out of the house while he and my father were playing some rowdy game together in the lounge, but my mother halted me as I slid my arms into my coat.

"We'll take care of him for the afternoon," she suggested, a note of warning in her voice. "Go and see some old friends. Why not? But your father tires easily these days. You must be back for Adrian by five."

I went and sat in the park a half hour's walk away, in the chill, sodden afternoon air, rocking myself on a swing that pressed its chains into my hips. Child-bearing hips, the kind no woman wants, even if she actually wants a child.

Which, personally, I did not.

I thought of getting on the train back to London, leaving the boy in my parents' care, but they'd only restore him to me like a forgotten glove.

My boy, beautiful and trusting and intolerable to be near. In his eyes I could see my own failings – perfect miniature replications, inverted and unforgivable. I couldn't bear to see my worst suspicions about myself reflected in his unflickering gaze. It's not much of an excuse, I know that now, but at the time it seemed fair enough. An unwanted child is a terrible thing. All children should be wanted by someone, shouldn't they? I felt I would simply be stepping aside, allowing people who genuinely craved him to take him into their lives, out of the cold.

As we ambled back to the train station, cutting through the park, he let out a cry of joy, darted ahead to a low, damp bench. A box stood on its boards, one corner of the lid raised up, one pink nose waffling through.

"Why has she leaved them?" he asked me, wonder in his accusatory eyes, but I didn't have an answer for that.

"Stay here," I said. "Play with them as much as you like." And I walked away, boarded the train, watched the countryside blur into green and brown ribbons beyond the window. I thought I saw the mouse woman sitting on the other side of the aisle, but I didn't want to meet her eyes in case she remembered me. In case she felt as I did and didn't want me to remember her.

*

Of course, he was found, safe as houses if a bit blue around the edges. He was taken in by a foster family while the social workers tried to figure out why I'd done it, while I shrugged and smiled and refused to meet their eyes.

I signed the paperwork, let them remove him neatly from my life, let them house me temporarily in a ward that smelled of old chips and window cleaning fluid. Let my parents tiptoe around me like they found me terrifying. Perhaps all parents fear their children, fear the truths they will see reflected back at them.

And when I re-entered the world, I was alone – empty and pure, like a clean water glass. Sometimes, I'd see my reflection in shop windows and I'd be smiling faintly, like someone concealing and relishing a private joy.

That's what made my husband fall for me, that secretive smile. He mistook it for a promise of good things underneath, when in truth I was smiling because I had the sense of having got away with something. I'd been presented with motherhood and had been able to pass it on as easily as a woman abandons a box of mice on a park bench.

I've kept up these weekly sessions, perhaps because I know, deep inside, that there's something very wrong with me. It may seem an extravagance, paying a stranger £80 to listen to me, but other than my aged mum this counsellor is the only person who knows the boy exists. Knows what I did.

Nearly thirty years of waiting for the guilt to hit, and all that's happened is that he's sent me an email asking for us to meet, and I've agreed.

I haven't been back to the town where I grew up since my father died, just months after I let the boy be taken from us. But it seems right to return now.

I think about another blessing; I have something to look forward to – a train journey to a Hampshire coastal town, and a walk to a park, to a bench where I'll sit and wait for the man who claims to be my boy to return.

Lodged

I T ' S J U S T A F T E R 5am when Graham comes to find me. I'm in the cellar, still in my pyjamas, one leg half over the old armchair that sits in the section where the landlord's dumped the former tenant's possessions. I pause when he comes in.

"Charlie, what are you doing?"

"Did I wake you?" I push my tangled hair out of my eyes with one hand. "Sorry. Couldn't sleep."

I've found all kinds of things: old paintings, teddy bears, dressmaking fabrics… I wave a blue gymkhana ribbon in the air, half amused, half aghast. "Why would anyone leave this stuff behind?"

"Charlie, I really don't think…" He hesitates. "She might come back for it, mightn't she? We can't just chuck it out."

"Yeah, I know." I grin at him, feeling like a mischievous child. "But don't you think it's intriguing? What kind of person collects this junk, and then leaves it behind? There's a lava lamp over there, and look at this crockery!"

"I once had a lava lamp," he reminds me. "When we were at uni that counted as mood lighting. And most people have plates. Can we go back to bed now?"

"You go, if you're tired," I say. "You need to get up for work in a few hours. But I don't, do I?"

That could have sounded like a jab, a reminder that it's for him I've moved here, for him I've left my job, my home.

"…and I'm wide awake now!" I continue, extra bright, blowing him a kiss.

People always move for love or money. I read that in a magazine somewhere, so it must be true. Graham moved for money, I moved for love. Well, in a way we both moved for love, hoping that a new home, a new view, would give us fresh eyes for each other. A change is as good as a holiday, I've heard. Better, in fact, because you don't have to wait around killing hours in airports.

Only, without a job to go to, I feel a bit aimless – unanchored.

Graham heads off for work at 8am, and for a while I sort of drift around the unfamiliar house that's now our home. Then I decide I need to be proactive, so I go through the jobs pages, phone four recruitment agencies, email my CV to a couple of companies.

That takes less than two hours, leaving most of the day still stretched ahead of me.

I take my time unpacking boxes, trying to find homes for our odds and ends – stupid things like cheese graters (why do we have more than one?) and stacks of old birthday cards. I take them out of their box and then get frozen by the uncertainty of whether we need to keep them at all.

At one point I go down to the cellar to stow away the empty boxes and accidentally knock over a crate. Amongst the things that spill out there's one of those plastic inhalers that asthmatics carry. I stand there, staring at it. Surely it's the kind of thing you need to keep with you?

Back upstairs I open the cupboard beneath the kitchen sink and find eight bottles of vodka queued up at the back of it. Three have been opened and drunk down a few inches. But why so many? And why store them under the sink when there are so many other cupboards to choose from?

When Graham gets home, I show him the bottle octet. He raises an eyebrow. "Maybe the old lodger was an alkie." He sets about tipping the contents of the open ones down the sink, saying, when I protest at the waste: "She could have done anything to them, Charlie, laced them with something…"

I feel a shiver go through me as I watch the liquid swirl down the drain, like the sorrow those bottles were supposed to dilute is welling up into the air instead, settling down over my head and shoulders.

Graham asks if I've been out today and I realise I haven't.

*

During the night the rhythmic drumming of rain against the skylight outside our room wakes me. I slip out of bed and sit cross-legged on the landing in the splodges of moonlight and cloud-shadows, letting the noise slide into my head.

I must doze right off, because when I open my eyes there's a woman sitting in front of me, head tilted to one side. She seems friendly enough, but a bit perplexed to find someone on her landing in the middle of the night.

When morning comes, I walk down the cellar steps and see that the space has flooded. The former tenant's poor teds are sitting in puddles of rainwater with their fur spiked in all directions. I find an old stripy jumper in one of the crates, so I bundle them up in it to stick in the washing machine. That way, at least when July comes for them, they'll be looking their best.

That's her name: July Winterson. I discovered it when a Horse & Pony magazine arrived for her in the post. Lovely name. I imagine her always in sunshine, getting ready to go for a ride on her most beloved horse. Such a cheerful image. It makes it impossible for me to believe she was an alcoholic, like Graham reckons.

"Stupid name," he sneers. "Maybe she was drinking to forget it."

I glare at him. "She might just be the type of person who enjoys inviting friends over for drinks. What's wrong with that?"

Still, I agree, it is odd, the way she's hidden vodka bottles throughout the house. When we go to shift the lopsided sofa that's slowly doing Graham's back in, there's a clunking noise. We carefully tip the sagging thing up on end and out roll three bottles of vodka. One of them smashes on the floor, making the place reek. Graham swears and scowls like the smell is assaulting his brain.

One other thing is bothering me – I keep hearing an odd wheezing sound. Something wrong with the pipes? I want to ask Graham what he thinks, but it'll be late when he gets home and he'll be knackered. This new job is eating most of his time.

I'm trying not to mind, trying to absorb myself in making the house nice and searching for work. Not that there seems to be any relevant vacancies out there anyway. I get the sense Graham thinks I'm not making a proper effort.

I miss the office I used to work in with Jan and Nick and Pat, just the four of us carrying out our own little tasks. Here in the city there only seem to be huge offices packed with people, and they don't need me.

Actually, I'm not sure Graham does either.

*

Some stupid woman from a recruitment agency rings and offers me a day's work in a call centre. If I'd picked up the phone I'd have told her that's my idea of hell, but Graham gets there first and says I'd love to do it. He drives me there, like he thinks I might not go otherwise. Like he suspects I'm not to be trusted.

I spend the morning surrounded by skinny teenagers phoning up old people and trying to hard-sell them things they've never heard of. I end up walking out just after midday, so I'm not sure I'll get paid.

It takes me an age to find my way back to the house, and by then I'm so distraught I need a good cry. I trail into the sanctuary of the cellar and sit on the dusty steps cuddled up in the stripy jumper I found down here a while ago.

When I finally stop sobbing, I notice that odd wheezing sound again.

I raise my head slowly, pulse jigging.

The woman from my dream is sitting in the dust at the far side of the cellar. She smiles at me, blinking her cat-like eyes, and I smile back. She's wearing a jumper that matches mine.

By the time Graham gets home I'm feeling pretty happy. I've even made a big veggie stew for us to eat together. Think he's giving himself the credit for getting me out of the house, and I can't see any reason to burst his bubble.

I leave a bowl of stew at the bottom of the stairs for July. Wonder if she'll be there again tomorrow.

*

Graham's working longer and longer hours, and when he is home he's worse than useless. Like on Sunday afternoon, when without saying a word he marches down to the cellar and starts sorting through boxes, preparing to throw half of it away.

I shout at him to leave it alone and he says, all annoying and calm, "Listen, Charlie, Julie Whatsherface won't be coming back for this old rubbish. We may as well get rid of it."

So I yell at him, "July, her name's July! At least have the courtesy to get her name right!"

"How am I supposed to remember a stranger's name?" he snaps. "I barely know yours these days, I see you so little."

Before I can ask him whose fault he thinks that is, he picks up a box stacked with toiletries. I try to grab it off him, and the cardboard tears, scattering July's possessions across the floor.

He tries to hug me while I'm scrabbling around, rescuing shampoos bottles, lotions and make up, but I shake him off. Why doesn't he understand that this matters?

"Don't you get it?" I ask. "Don't you get that this is wrong? No women would leave these kind of things behind. Something bad must have happened."

He gives up then, flings his hands in the air and tells me to keep the stuff if it means so much to me.

I've taken to wearing one of the perfumes that was in the box, something sweet and comforting. Graham says I don't even smell like myself any more.

It's better when he's not here. That's what July says, and I agree. We don't need him. We cosy up together in the cellar on a heap of July's old dressmaking materials and she tells me stories to make me giggle. It's damp down here, but I'm snug in the striped jumper and July's arms. Sometimes she gets a bit morose, which worries me, but she just curls up beside me, head in my lap like a cat.

One afternoon I move a packing case and discover a dark blemish not far from the bottom of the stairs. I want to ask her about it but she looks appalled – sort of brittle and transparent. I quickly cover it over again; cradle her in my arms till she stops trembling.

Later, I go upstairs to put something in the oven for dinner, and catch sight of myself in the hall mirror – face smudged, hair and eyes wild – not at all like myself.

I go into the bathroom to clean myself up for Graham, but just as I put in the plug and turn on the hot tap, the phone rings. He's letting me know he'll be home late. Again.

What if he's having an affair?

The words appear in my mind as if they're my own, but when I glance in the mirror, sure enough, there she is, cat-like eyes brimming with compassion.

I've left some love for you here, behind the tub, she tells me. That's what she calls her bottles of vodka.

Love. Clear and uncomplicated and just a little bit burning hot.

I slide into the steaming water, bottle in hand, and let July love me.

*

"I don't think I can do this any more." That's what he says. "It isn't that I don't love you, but these days I'm not sure I know you." Then he mutters, so I barely hear him: "You're becoming a stranger."

Rude man. That's July's name for him: The Rude Man Who Should Move Out.

I overhear him on the phone one evening, talking about me to god only knows who. His new girlfriend? "I think she might be drinking," he squawks. "Sometimes I can smell something sharp over the stink of that awful flowery perfume."

He pauses for a moment, presumably while his other woman slags me off.

"And whenever I come home, she gives me evils like I'm intruding. I think she wants me to go. Like, properly leave."

It's taken him long enough to get the hint.

Soon after, he sits down beside me on the cellar steps and mumbles on and on. I tune him out and listen to July murmuring sweet nothings in my head instead. He grabs my shoulders suddenly, making me jump, and July screeches in panic at me to get away, to run for my life. I hear him shouting my name as I sprint up the stairs. His cheek is crimson where I've smacked him.

On leaving day, I sit in the bedroom by the window so I can watch as he carries his bags to the car. He comes back upstairs and stands in the doorway, blinking at me all sad and bewildered.

He walks into the room, crouches on the carpet right in front of me, and I stare at him.

"Charlie," he says, lifting one hand like he wants to cup my cheek. I turn to the wall. "Charlie, just say the word. If you ask me to stay, I'll stay."

I can hear July chanting in my ear: Tell him to go. Tell the Rude Man to go...

I nod, then scowl as I see his eyes widen with misplaced hope. "You're not wanted here, Graham," I spit, and I can taste the venom in my voice. Graham clearly hears it too – I see him shiver minutely and feel bad for a moment, until July's damp, adoring breath envelops me.

"Go on, Graham, get out," I snarl. "We don't need you anyway."

He blinks at me, and stands up. "If I were you, I'd go to the doctor about that wheeze in your chest – doesn't sound good," he says softly. Then he's gone and the door slams shut behind him.

Good riddance.

I moved here for love, didn't I? And that's exactly what I've found. Tucked in every alcove, in each shadowy corner, a pair of cat-like eyes and a smile just for me.

Invertebrates

WE DUG HER up each solstice; each time she was a little lighter, her joints a little more unhinged. I worried she might come apart entirely, sinew and bones giving way as we propped her in the place of honour.

My brother and I allowed the invertebrates that had made her their home to attend our celebrations too. Sometimes centipedes fell from her eye-sockets and throat cavity to roam among the feast. I watched beetles nestle into her breastbone, and recalled how comfortably my head once rested there.

I took care to check every forkful for wriggles before raising it to my mouth. Spiders laced webs over the bread rolls, but they weren't for eating anyway.

It was harder earlier on, when remnants of flesh still clung to her ribs. The stench of rot invaded my nostrils till I could barely keep down the roast lamb, potatoes and beans that my brother had prepared.

Now her scent was of earthy loam – far more palatable.

I wondered if the change in smell meant she was fully departed at last, and we'd soon be able to leave her in peace.

My brother was the one who'd insisted on this ritual – our biannual commemoration of the captor we'd almost come to love.

We crooned the lullabies and folk songs she'd woven through our childhoods, and I recited the poems and parables she'd taught me. I remembered how I used to squirm in her lap when I was small, seeking the comfort of her heat whenever I missed our mum.

My brother raised a glass and we toasted the woman who'd caged us, protected us, tried to fatten us. Candle flames shivered on their wicks, and her skull gleamed like the moon, faint fissures mirroring lunar seas. The cracks were blackened from the fire we'd burnt her in.

Before dawn came we carried her back to the forest and the grave we'd interred, breaking up the bread rolls as we went – a symbolic reminder of the trail of crumbs that had failed to lead us home.

We tucked in limb and digit, layering on the soil till she was covered. I made sure we buried each insect and worm with her in the rich, dark earth.

When we turned to leave, duty complete for another six months, I felt relief unwind in my spine.

Geese Among the Trees

I SEE IT from the train each day, nestled between the fields and the canal. If I'm travelling at dusk or the day is overcast and stormy, the windows glint against the stone walls. I can imagine you then, moving about in there, doing whatever it is that you do without me. Or perhaps you're resting your elbows against a window ledge looking out, wearing a worn-thin, oversized jumper, watching the train zipping by like something fleeing through the landscape, headed god knows where – who cares where as long as it's away?

Away from the house we shared – the one and a half rooms downstairs, two and a half up, if you counted the loft where the bats lodged and paid rent in foul-smelling droppings.

"Guano," you told me, and scooped it up to fertilise the garden, transforming it into carrots and lettuces – a kind of alchemy. I never could eat them without feeling squeamish, although I knew they'd been scrubbed clean.

Country living, it's not for everyone.

At first it was an adventure. We laughed at the ferns snaking in through the window frames and marvelled at the leopard-spotted slugs in our damp-mottled bathroom. We cooed over the chest of moth-eaten jumpers you found in the bat loft; you settled down with thread and needles, embroidering crimson hearts to draw each ragged hole closed.

"You're a manbroiderer," I teased you, and you told me your grandmother had taught you to sew. I tried to imagine how that must feel, to hold memories of someone sitting beside you quietly demonstrating how to thread the needle, weave the empty spaces through with stem stitch, feather stitch, buttonhole stitch – incantations to keep wear and tear at bay.

Each morning we surfaced to sunlight dappling the canal,

trickling through the branches of the abandoned orchard. You linked your fingers through mine, led me outside, dragged off your boots and socks, and stood there, toes wriggling joyfully in the dew-damp grass.

As I hesitated, you knelt at my feet, unlaced my trainers; slipped them free. The moment when you cradled one of my heels in the palm of your hand made me shiver inside. I felt you were accepting me for me, not just for my pretence. It frightened me, but thrilled me too, silently, to my core.

We were happy, weren't we? For a time at least. Or was I kidding myself, and you, playing the role of the person that I wished I could be?

In truth I was a city-girl at heart, my heart itself as shrivelled as a forgotten walnut still in its coat of blackened fruit. It surprises me how long I managed to hide it from you. Or was it that you made me forget? Forget myself, and so become someone better. For a time at least.

I lost so much, you see, when I was young. So much that I grew lost. People found me and then forgot me; gave up on me. That erodes a child, and erosion is scary when you're all you have. You think that one day you'll wake to discover that what little remains of you has crumbled into the sea and been swept away.

So you build defences to protect yourself, develop hard skins around your tender parts, and try to lock away the piece of you that tends to forget, tends to accidentally care. That most vulnerable of parts.

When we met, that particular bit of me couldn't help but be drawn to you, fluttering helplessly towards your transparency: your eager, open happiness.

And this house, where you flung open each door like you were unveiling some great treasure, completed the illusion. I loved you, and so I loved it, or at least the idea of loving you and it.

My charade couldn't last forever. The snickering childhood voices began making themselves known even as we waltzed barefoot together among the bruised fruit, mocking and reviling, crying out "watch out for wasps!" until I lost my nerve, stopped mid-spin, pulled my hand from yours and raced into the house.

Where the snickerers found other things to mock, calamities to thrill against, spiked with bitter glee.

I ignored them as stubbornly as I could, but it was they who woke me to listen to the trains humming past in the darkness, cocked my ear to your snoring, made me recoil from your morning breath. Nudged me into an obsession with picking the sharp goose feather stalks from the pillows as you pressed your slick flesh into me.

Flicking them free.

Who builds paradise within earshot of a railway?

One morning you called out from the kitchen for me to "come and see!" Still blinking away the porridge-thick sludge of dreams, I shuffled downstairs, pulling one of the embroidered jumpers over my bare skin. You ushered me to the open door where sunbeams refracted through the green and blue.

A flock of geese had arrived while we slept and now grazed, shimmering white, between the trees. The way you responded to the sight was like a child to a conjuring trick, to a herd of unicorns.

Your childhood must have been full of magic. Crammed with possibilities that now leaked from you as hope, anticipation: existence shored up by optimism.

I knew then that I had to leave.

Optimism is as dangerous as disappointment, can just as easily erode your defences. I packed a bag while you were outside chatting with the geese. When you made your way into the village to buy apples, milk, bread, I set off in the opposite direction, towards the railway tracks.

My farewell note simply stated: "I'm less than you think I am. Sorry."

Time has passed. The city has given me the anonymity I craved, and the chance to reinvent, rewrite, to re-emerge as someone stronger, better able to cope with both disappointment and hope. I sit here in my smart shoes, smart suit, my bright blue leather satchel on my knee and know the note I left you was not entirely true.

I can see now that I'd underestimated myself, and you. I know now that I should have written: "I am not who you think I am, but maybe, given time, I can be."

I slip my hand into my pocket; find the hand-stitched heart I keep there, snipped from that jumper before I fled.

I hold it in my palm, as light as goose down, and think about writing to you in your small house. I imagine you holding the envelope in your hand. Remembering the geese among the trees.

The Blue Suitcase

I'M LOOKING OUT for mine, I really am, hoping and hoping it will be next, but then I spy it, a little blue case bouncing jauntily along the conveyor belt. I can't help myself – I just... reach out.

I don't know what makes me do it. It doesn't resemble mine in the slightest. Bella is sobbing and squirming in my arms, it's too hot with everyone crowded around the luggage carousel, and it takes forever for the first weary bags to roll into view.

Somehow I feel like this is the suitcase I've been waiting for.

The handle fits comfortably in my palm, as though it's chosen me. I lift the case onto the shiny floor of the arrivals hall with one hand, hold Bella securely in my other arm, and march smartly away.

In the lift to the long-stay car park, I beam at Bella and confide, "That's not my suitcase. It's too perfect!" in exactly the tone I read her favourite book to her. She chuckles obligingly, and I beam.

I still don't know why Keith suggested I drive myself to the airport. The parking fees are extortionate and money is nearly always his big bugbear. Maybe he couldn't bear to think of one of our friends bringing me instead and wanting to know what was wrong and where I was going with the baby.

I buckle Bella into her seat and pop open the boot to slide the case in, but the space is so big and dark and the case so neat and bright that my resolve quails.

Instead I lie the case on the passenger seat beside me. Throughout the drive home I keep noticing it out of the corner of my eye: a splash of blue glimmering up at me.

Keith's car isn't parked in our cul-de-sac, although it's after six and I'm certain I texted him the time our flight got in.

I consider phoning, but what if he's in a meeting with clients?

I don't want him to catapult straight into resentment after we've been apart for almost a month.

After so much time away, I find myself assessing our home with fresh eyes, noting the scuffs the walls where Kevin has been careless with his golfing equipment, and the ugly outdated dido rails I've been wanting to remove since the day we moved in.

I feed Bella and then search the cupboards and fridge for something to eat myself, eventually making myself a sandwich from ham, stale bread and lettuce that may be well over three weeks old. I can't believe he hasn't had time to go to the supermarket in the time Bella and I have been gone.

The case is still standing patiently by the door, its blue vivid against our dull off-white walls and smudge-grey carpet. "I should unpack, shouldn't I?" I say to Bella and she babbles her agreement.

I wheel it into the lounge, put Bella in her bouncy chair and place the case in front of her. She goes "Ooh," and claps her hands like she did when she saw the sea sparkling outside Mum's apartment block.

The luggage tag has a name written on it in curling letters, *Chloe Gatestable*, but no contact details.

"Shall we see what's inside?" I ask Bella, and she coos softly.

It's the direct opposite of my own chaotically stuffed luggage. Row upon row of rolled garments nestle tidily in place.

One by one, I ease them out: vests, shorts, skirts, sundresses and bikinis. They're high quality, beautifully made, and breathtakingly carefree. I drag off my travel-stale jeans and a t-shirt that appears to have the remains of Bella's lunch glued to the front. In their place, I slip on a skirt, then try a dress, and then a pair of butter-coloured shorts. I twirl and spin, admiring my new, feminine wardrobe, while Bella applauds in approval. Such a flattering fit – they could have been bought with me in mind. The bikini tops and vests are a teensy bit tight, but I suspect the case's former owner isn't lactating daily.

Not one item seems designed with the demands of a baby in mind. It reminds me of the person I used to be, which saddens me momentarily. I lift Bella out of her chair and give her a good squeeze before putting her down so I can root deeper into the case.

A camera sits tucked inside a wide-brimmed sun hat. It isn't especially expensive-looking, but there's something pleasing about its weight in my hand. I slump onto the sofa, wearing a flared mini skirt and my own old greying bra, and click through the photos.

Hilltops dotted with vineyards and olives, secluded coves and a smiling man with teeth gleaming in the sun... This is the Greece beyond the retirement village, beyond earshot of my mum dispensing advice like liquid soap.

"If you don't trust Keith, make him look you in the eye and ask him straight – are you having an affair?"

"I did, Mum. I did do that."

Mum drew her sunglasses down her nose, eyes shrewd. "Darling, did you truly?" Her gaze locked onto mine until I felt my retinas burn.

"Ok, not quite, but..."

"I've never seen you, or Keith, confront anyone. You're not argumentative types. I'll bet the pair of you never had a blazing argument in your whole marriage. That's what you need to do – shout out your grievance and clear the air!"

I didn't tell her about the girl I'd seen him kiss at that party, or rather, in his words, the girl who'd chosen to kiss him. As though being the kissee rather than the kisser exonerated him. But, as I pointed out in measured tones the next day, no girl puts herself out there without some indication her advances would be welcomed.

"You think that because you don't have an impetuous bone in your body," he replied. "Don't believe all women are like you."

That afternoon I booked the flights to Greece. How's that for impetuous?

When he'd prised his lips from the woman's, Keith was flushed and gasping. I can't remember the last time he responded to one of my kisses like that.

I glance at the clock – past 7.30pm. On my phone, I find a text from the network welcoming us home, but still no word from Keith. As far as he's concerned, we should have landed far earlier. It was the delay at Athens that made us so late.

I press the button to speed-dial his number.

"You've reached Keith Morgan's phone. I'm unavailable right now but if you leave a message with your name and number I'll get back to you."

He sounds cheerful, not in the slightest like a man desperately missing his wife and child.

Sighing, I flick through more photos, pausing at one showing the man with a woman, presumably Chloe. They're standing thigh-deep in an azure sea, laughing behind snorkelling masks. She's wearing an emerald green bikini I already discarded as too tight at the bust. Such a pretty, happy girl.

I try to swallow my resentment but it's drier than my ham sandwich from earlier.

There they are sipping cocktails against a Pinterest-perfect sunset, and here, kayaking. I've always wanted to try kayaking. Envy throbs inside me. How come she gets to be blissfully liberated? And how dare she rub that in my face?

I shiver, aware suddenly that it's growing dark outside and I'm half-naked in our living room. A promising fluffy cream corner beckons me – an invitation. I give it a wrench and it flaps out, unfolding into a sumptuous shawl. With it flies something slim and rectangular that careers into the air, plummets and skids across the rug.

I scoop it up with trembling fingers, whispering apologies.

A notepad. No, a sketchpad, crammed with tiny drawings of Greek islands. "Look, Bella! Oh, aren't they good?"

And at the front, a message in the same, looping handwriting as on the luggage tag: "If found, please return to Chloe Gatestable, 59 Clifton Way…"

Just the other side of town.

I stare at it.

Bella, perhaps sensing the change of mood in the room, starts to cry. I wipe my sweating palms on the grubby beige sofa cushions, and try soothing her, jiggling her, rocking her… She weeps on unrelentingly.

"Where's your dummy?" I ask, but know she must have lost it. She manages to lose them despite me tying them to her clothing.

Where are the spares? Oh, yes, in the battered, unclaimed suitcase that's probably still sliding around the luggage carousel.

Unless it has already been blown up by airport security.

I find that I'm smiling, imagining those tired belongings exploding in a puff of fire and smoke. And here – look – a fresh start shining right in front of me. If I chose to, I could pile everything back into the case and drive off into the night with Bella.

Keith would be none the wiser. Better, surely, than struggling on with a marriage neither of us seems willing to put our energy into. We barely made contact while I was in Greece. And he hasn't bothered to welcome us home.

It's Bella's grizzling that makes up my mind. If nothing else, a drive might settle her.

I heap vests, shorts, skirts, sundresses and bikinis, camera and sketchpad into the sky-blue case, caress the shawl regretfully and fold it on top. Then I zip the suitcase closed, pick up Bella and head out to the car.

Rain dapples the windscreen, gilded by the headlights. Bella drops off to sleep before we exit the cul-de-sac, leaving me alone with the sound of rain and the subdued blue of the suitcase.

I consider driving towards the motorway and onwards into the night, but the luggage tag dangles in the periphery of my vision, sort of waving at me with the engine's thrum. I let my impulses guide me to 59 Clifton Way.

It feels eerie to pull up outside her house. I feel I'm being offered a further glimpse of the life denied to me. Open curtains reveal an attractive interior in tasteful shades of cream and honeyed wood – precisely what I might have imagined for her.

I spot a movement through a window near the rear of the property. I don't know what makes me do it; I get out of the car, into the rain, and run right across the lawn, coming to a halt in the shadow of a beech tree.

The argument Chloe and her boyfriend are having is of a type I've only previously seen on TV – loud and vigorous, punctuated by accusatory pointing. They'd been on the same flight as me, suffered the same laborious delays, waited in the same hot, crowded arrivals hall, and when every other piece of luggage had been claimed, they'd found themselves left with my ugly, discarded suitcase.

Not much of a fair swap, if I'm honest.

I could have been brave, I know, but I have a baby in the car, and I'm not sure how I'd explain myself. I slide the case from the passenger seat, lug it up to the top of the steps and give the doorbell two long loud blasts to make sure they hear over their shouting. Then I race down the steps and throw myself into the car. Speed away.

I'm not sure why, but something about the whole thing makes me laugh out loud. With Bella still fast asleep in her car seat, I dial Keith's mobile number. I think I'm about ready for that blazing row.

Part Three

Rain

Distant Storms

WHEN THE FLOODS came, most people stuck it out for a time, then lost their nerve and travelled beyond the outer reaches of the city, seeking higher ground. Not us. We stayed put in the tower block, watching as the streets went under, and then the bridges and even the skyscrapers closest to the strand. You showed me how to fish from the windows, going up a floor each month as the water levels climbed. We learnt to swim through the murky waves, salvaging anything that floated, diving down through waterlogged buildings to rescue anything we could make use of.

It's almost a decade since anyone came by. When the smoke went up, a bruised ribbon against the sky, hope sprang within me. I watched you paddle off in the kayak, caution etched into your spine.

You told me you'd be back before dusk.

That was six months ago.

I decorate our home with bunting made from salvaged shredded dresses and shiny blue-black cormorant feathers to show you when you return. Clouds swell overhead and lightning scars the horizon. I hear the sigh of waves collapsing into each other's arms and pretend they're voices approaching.

I wonder what I'll do if one day I'm right.

The Sculptor

S HE HAS TO pause every hour – that's what the orthopaedist advised – to take a break from the frozen quiet and ease warmth back into her body. Standing in the studio, Isha cradles a steaming mug close to her throat so that the licking fingers of vapour lap at her chin. She feels the quietness inside her soften and begin to melt.

Even the juddering growl of the chainsaw can't disperse the peace that takes hold while she's working. She feels it grip her interior like the shy fingers of ghosts. Isha wonders how much time she has left before the orthopaedist's caution makes itself known. The cold can get into your bones, cause issues later on, more so when coupled to the chainsaw's boisterous vigour.

Ironic, somehow, to discover medical truth in the age-old warning.

She must have heard it a thousand times as a teenager – her mum calling her back for a jacket: "You'll catch your death!" And her dad: "Do as she asks, love. She'll only worry otherwise."

His keen insights ingrained in compassion as always.

It's still in there now, the insight, she's sure of it; simply shrouded by the gloaming of semantic dementia. Hoar frost clouding synapses that used to flare as bright as the sun.

"You think too much." That's Elkie – housemate, friend – though it sounds like something her dad might once have said. "Too much time alone with stupid blocks of ice. You need to come out with me, meet people who can talk back." Then adding: "Who you haven't carved yourself."

Wise words, for sure, but what Elkie doesn't grasp, what Isha herself barely understands, is that the people she digs out of the ice don't need to talk, because they listen. Even before their faces emerge, she feels they can hear her thoughts, help her to sort through her emotions – layers of salt-crusted shells on a beach.

The first time her dad attended an exhibition where her work was on show, she'd seen wonderment in his eyes. "Reminds me of a pillar of salt," he exclaimed, then grinned. "Ice would melt the salt, though."

"Other way round, Dad," she'd murmured, but not so loud he'd hear.

Correcting him seemed needlessly cruel. He wouldn't retain the amendment anyway – it would just momentarily shame him with the realisation he'd gone wrong. Was increasingly going wrong.

Once when she visited, he had a friend with him, a man he'd worked with. They were similar ages but her dad looked far older now, hunched by the absences being carved by the progressive condition.

"Ah, here's my younger!" he'd said to his friend, who rose to shake her hand.

"How are you, Isha? Your old man says you have a new job."

"I'm well," she said, aware she was using the soft, warm tones she always engaged around her dad these days, as though he was an animal she didn't want to risk spooking. "Not new, really. It's been a few years."

"She takes great blocks of life!" her dad interjected. "Makes them, bakes them? Takes them into shape."

"I'm an ice sculptor," she told his former colleague, who nodded his appreciation.

"How interesting! For corporate functions?"

"Sometimes," she said, abashed as always when discussing her creations. "More often fine art."

"For galleries?" He'd been impressed. "Gosh, all that effort. Doesn't it make you sad when they melt away?"

People often ask that, not understanding that the higher end establishments purchase refrigerated units for her work, while others consider the degradation part of the art.

For Isha, the purpose lies in the making itself. Discovering the design, then easing it out, first with a chainsaw, then with increasingly small and precise chisels. She watched a film recently, a heist movie, in which one of the team was a safe breaker. As he tapped the safe's door, listening for the sound that would direct him one way or another, she found that she identified with his actions. It's what she does when preparing to work on a piece of ice – seeking the sculpture that rests within its cloudy frozen flesh.

It's almost impossible to express that to anyone who doesn't do it, and she's yet to meet another artist currently working in her field, with her particular, chilly material.

She shivers suddenly. Shakes herself free from her ponderings – there, another of her father's words. He always called her his little ponderer, would shout from the doorway: "Come on, little pon, we're off for a tramp round the woods. Got to get the blood moving!"

She smirks at the memory, too cold to outright grin. He's right, and Elkie is too – she needs to venture out more, step into rooms where blood pulses; laughter and chatter rising rather than exhalations smoking into frozen air.

As she cycles home to the flat, she wonders if she's lonely. Most of her work is accomplished alone – the only time a group is needed is when she requires a new block to work on and brings together a team to position the next vast cube shipped in especially.

That's something else people don't comprehend. "It can't be just any old ice," she tells the boy at the party, the one Elkie has introduced her to, shoving them together with determination fierce in her smile. Isha's aware of the fervour in her voice; tries to soften the edges of her words. "It must be strong right through – flawless. Normal ice hides air bubbles that'd show up as a hole at just the wrong point."

Like the one spreading where her dad's deftness with language once sat, she thinks but doesn't say.

Perhaps this is the thing that gnaws at her – not loneliness as such, but a sense of loss for the father who loved to joke and tell riddles, teach her about the world with a luminosity of language as radiant as the prism that hung from the window when she was tiny; refracting light into rainbows that bounced around her room.

One long ago winter, a row of icicles appeared. Each day as spring crept near, they dripped a little, shrank a little, until they disappeared.

"Where'd they go?" she'd wanted to know, and her father laughed.

"They're still here, Isha, just in another form. Ice melts into water, then water evaporates into vapour – drifts into the air."

He taught her that nothing is ever truly lost, not entirely.

She pictures that often: ice becoming water becoming something able to fly. A kind of magic.

"What do you love about it," the boy asks, bringing her back to him. She sees that he's genuinely interested. She looks at his hands, one holding a glass of beer, the other by his side.

The block she is working on is pristine milky bluish white, almost whole. How to explain the excitement of that, and the anticipation? She focuses on the details, tells the boy how she dresses as though preparing to hike across snowfields, to climb a mountain to its diamond-capped heights. "When I first started out, it frightened me how heavy the chainsaw felt, how loud it was," she admits. "Now it's an extension of me, and when it roars into life the sound's... It's just another of *my* sounds, you know, like my breath, the way your blood sounds in your head..." She flounders, but the boy is steady, nodding as he takes in her words. She glances at his hands again and reaches out, touches the free one. The warmth of his skin beneath her fingertips is pleasing. She can feel a smooth streak where no hair grows; the aftermath of a burn. She feels the urge to let him examine her own hands; discover the faint pattern of injuries incurred early on in her career, when she was less careful.

Part of her misses those days, she realises. When it was still shining and new, before she grew into one of the foremost practitioners of her artform.

She talks about how she lets her mind loosen, envision the figure she wants to see emerge from the ice – the posture, the features.

She watches the boy as she speaks. Elkie pointed him out so quickly Isha knows she'd had this in mind all along, had picked him out for her. What's his name? Simon? No, Sean, that's it.

When she subsides into silence, he waits a moment, and then begins to describe his own work as a glass blower. How the tongs grow white hot when he uses them to grip the neck of whatever vessel he's shaping. "I love the idea that the glass was once grains of sand, just lying on a beach, and that I'm able to transform them so utterly," he says, and smiles in a way that makes his eyes glimmer.

The next day, in the freezer, she can't stop seeing his gaze, even as she completes the early strokes of the sculpture, carving great sweeps of ice that feather around the base. Now she must concentrate fully, shove thoughts of the boy aside as she moves closer and deeper into the ice, swapping tool for tool, growing increasingly exact. She picks out the limbs, torso, each foot and hand, and finally the lips, chin, temples, lashes. Until she has cut away the excess ice.

Set him free.

A portrait of her father, perhaps an homage. The museum trustees who commissioned the sculpture have purchased a climate-controlled cabinet that will display the statue while preserving it; preventing it from melting beyond recognition. The irony makes her shudder fractionally, almost causes her to chip his nose, but she holds the angled blade steady.

There will be a special unveiling of the sculpture, a black-tie event with patrons and media invited. Isha intends to take her dad along. She wonders if he will know himself, standing in that cabinet, frozen in time.

She thinks it may be the last time he's well enough to attend. Social occasions faze her father now. Forgetting the names of things is married to forgetting the things themselves. She has seen him marvel at a glass of water, unsure of its purpose. Fright jolts within him at times now, as the world's enigmas grows increasingly difficult to unpick.

She looks at the sculpture critically, and knows that the eyes are slightly wrong.

No one else would notice. The brow is her father's, and the apples of his cheeks, but the eyes themselves are less deep-set, younger. They're his, Sean's, the pupils and irises of the boy who seems to have taken up residence in her head.

When they met, she felt that there was a sorrow in him too – perhaps a form of prolonged grief like her own – but she also recognises a deep-rooted joy. Sean, too, finds serenity in what he does. More than that, she believes he has a gift for happiness. Isha wonders about that, wonders if she can match that delight.

She thinks she might want to find that out for herself.

Underwire

THE PEBBLES OF the beach are cold lumps beneath my soles. A January wind whistles in from the sea, but I ignore the goosebumps sprigging my flesh and with effort I think the core of me into heat. That's a trick, imagining an inferno lit at the centre of my gut, flames licking the ropes of intestines and keeping me warm.

The whole world is dressed in shades of bruises today – bluish pebbles, the greenish sea, a sky like slabs of ice above.

I glance up the beach; see the violet trim of my sneakers where I kicked them off a few steps back. Nearby, my socks lounge untidily like patches of lichen or moss. There's a café just beyond them, shutters closed for the season. No egg butties or cones of chips today. My head swims for a moment; hands rigid by my sides.

The next layer to come off is my fleece – a satisfying zip downwards – then my thin t-shirt crumples into a heap at my feet. Even with my bra still on, my nipples are instantly erect and alarmed. I run my fingers up the teeth of my ribcage, comforted by their protrusions.

The bra is just two triangles of fabric; the kind of thing a preteen girl might wear before developing a need for underwire.

It's not as if I ever got the support I wanted anyway.

I grimace and sit down to fumble with my belt catch. It seems to take forever to pull the length of leather from the loops of my jeans. Removing the jeans themselves requires some contortions. They bag around my ankles as I stand unsteadily and step aside.

The wind feels stronger now; it's a struggle to stay upright.

My knickers flap against the pale flesh of my inner thighs. They're gauzy black embroidered with pink roses. My best underwear, meant for nights of sizzling romance, long before I gave up on all that.

I unclasp my bra and let the wind ribbon it away.

Watching it swoop off like the tail of a kite, I remember how different this beach is in summer – crowded with couples and children and dogs; pools brimming with clear briny water where anemones and hermit crabs thrive.

Rolled up, the knickers fit neatly into a crevice at the throat of a barnacled rock.

There are caves at the edge of the shore where waves lap. When storms encroach, I've heard that they fill with ocean, becoming something other than themselves.

The heat inside me sputters quietly out – no longer necessary. Instinctively, I crouch low: spine curved, elbows and knees sharply angled. Calcium carbonate whispers over my vulnerable skin. With my eyes tight shut, I smile at the sense of being cradled in a layer of shell as brilliant red as fire.

My beautiful exoskeleton spreads and connects, covering the soft tissue that remains, and shielding every inward part of me from the world.

Breathing Water

THE MOON IS thin, casting a faint spool of light that catches in the waves beyond the harbour wall. Gil likes this kind of night, softened by the salt in the warm air, all colours subdued. He pads down to the dock, strips off his t-shirt and shorts, clambers down the steel steps welded to the wall. The metal is cold against his skin, but not, he knows, as cold as the sea itself will be, even here in the harbour where it has been quieted.

He enters slowly, allowing the chill to creep over his skin. Become the blood in his veins. He sinks until his ears are submerged, and exhales with something like relief. There, now not only the sights are muted, but the noises too. All except those he creates himself, which sound distinct and pure.

He swims across the harbour to the first shadowy hull, heaves himself on board and stands, shivering. The deck is slick beneath his feet, still wearing a residue of yesterday's catch. Gil pauses a moment, then reaches into the small bag hanging at his throat, takes the first shell his fingers touch and slips it behind a bundle of ropes – out of sight. He glances around, checks he is alone, unseen, then drops neatly over the side into the water's embrace.

*

He's almost full grown, but he can still fit into spaces where no one will notice him. He did that on the afternoon before last. The sun had crept between the garden shed and the wall of the house, and he'd followed its rays.

That's where he'd been when his mother was tending to the broad beans, and his father, Leonard, arrived at her elbow. He had paint on his hands like bruises. It reminded Gil of when he was five or six and his father still boxed on Thursday nights; how his mother would tend to his injuries, tsking soft under her breath.

"He's been at it again, Morwenna."

"Who, love?" Gil's mother asked, although Gil had guessed and was sure she must know too.

"Gil, of course." Leonard rolled his shoulders, as he used to before a fight, or after a full day's painting, loosening up the tendons. "Been sneaking onto the boats, it's not right, Mor!"

Gil listened; limbs pressed to the rough-smooth slats of the shed's rear. In the corners above him spiders sat cloaked in clots of web.

"What harm does it do, love? He's not damaging things, is he?" He doesn't know why she asked that. She must know he wouldn't, not her boy.

He peeked at his parents, intent on each other.

"No, he's... He's leaving shells again. Matty told me." Leonard grimaced, eyes narrowed. "Making a laughing stock of himself."

"Since when have you cared what that bunch think?" She smiled. "You didn't care when Matty and the others wanted you to go on the boats, did you? Didn't care when they mocked you for setting up the gallery, becoming an artist."

"I was tougher than Gil is."

"You can't protect him forever, love. The shells are part of his way of feeling in control," she said, "just like you with the boxing, and you stopped that, didn't you, when you didn't need it anymore?"

Leonard harrumphed. "It's not the same."

Morwenna looked at him. "Really? Do you believe that?"

His father had stepped away from his mother then and shambled off towards the house.

Gil emerged from his hiding place. "Low blow," he said to his mum.

"Not my fault he's faded," she retorted, laughing. "Poor man's not the fighter he was. And he knows I'm right."

*

Gil walks the shore just after sun-up, eyes searching. There'll be at least twelve boats in the harbour tonight, maybe more. He needs enough shells to anchor them, not to the quayside, but in this world, prevent each sinking through or arching up, dragging its crew out of life. He's seen it happen – vessels smashed to tinder, all souls lost.

The shells, though, they can avert that, he's certain of it.

It's something Uncle Matty said, that day when the squall hit, when they were out beyond the bay in the open sea and Gil had been certain they were going to die.

Uncle Matty had gritted his teeth, said, "Chin up, Gillion, we've got enough salt water here without your tears!"

And when he proceeded to blubber, his uncle held out an unsteady hand and pulled a periwinkle from behind his ear.

"Tahdah!"

There, magic.

Gil loved him for that instant.

It made sense to Gil that the tiny, yolk-yellow shell was the reason they'd made it back to shore unscathed.

And then, as the fears of the world grew in size and number and intensity, he reasoned with himself, perhaps not only that particular periwinkle was magic, but all of them, all seashells. It made him feel less panicked, less vulnerable, so he took that reasoning and made it fact, and now holds fast to it like a barnacle to a rock.

He works swiftly, searching the tideline, picking up each shell that catches his eye, then weighing it in his hands. He's listening for the resonance, the subtle vibration, that mean this is a good one, will do the trick. Some fail this simple test, and he cascades them into the kelp that lies in stinking ribbons at his feet, to nestle with mermaids' purses crisping black and brittle in the sun's rays.

When the fabric bag at his throat is full enough that the shells jostle, he retreats into a low cave where the shadows cradle him into the sleep he misses at night. The dreams that come lap gently, the creak of boats soothing the edge of his hearing.

He dreams of the day of his diagnosis, how little it mattered to him, and how much to his parents. How Morwenna gazed at him with such trepidation that he permitted her to cup his cheek with her hand, just for a moment.

How Leonard's shoulders had slumped, and how he'd barked at the doctor: "Now what? Is there a course of treatment? Can he be cured?"

"No," the doctor had said. "No, there's no cure, but there are ways… he can integrate into society better."

And later he'd heard them arguing, Morwenna saying sharply, "They wanted to cure you, did you forget that? Your brother and the rest wanted to cure you of your art!"

"That's different."

"But I don't think it is, Leonard," Morwenna had said in her quiet, powerful way. "I don't think it is at all."

*

Gil wakes late in the afternoon and heads towards home, passing the gallery where he sees Leonard standing, brush in hand, filling a canvas with waves. His father frowns as he glances from his work-in-progress to the bay, struggling with the effort of transforming something defined by its motion into painted stillness. He raises his eyes, sees Gil, and each nods, then carries on. Gil thinks of what Morwenna says, about them being more alike than either of them knows, and he wonders if it's true.

He remembers how his father, following the diagnosis, put one hand close to his arm. Almost touching but not quite. "Gil," he'd said, soft, an urgency in his voice like he had to spill his words before they disappeared. "Gil, you're going to need to be brave. Do you know what brave is? It's letting yourself be seen, however much you want to hide."

He hadn't known at the time, or for a long time afterwards, what Leonard meant.

The fishing boats are back, glistening catches shuddering. Gil blinks his gladness to see Uncle Matty in the midst of it, face reddened by wind and sun. Everyone has returned, safe.

"Hoi, Gil," the man hollers as he nears.

Gil pauses, uncertain from the tone whether he's in trouble or not. "Hi Uncle Matty."

"Take these to your mam, eh?"

The mackerel fly at him, dappled silver and gold, rebound off his chest and flop onto the harbour path still fluttering. He recoils as his uncle guffaws, the other men joining him. The noise feels threatening.

His t-shirt is smeared with scales. He whips them off and looks down at the fish, trying to ignore the way they're gulping, searching for water to breathe through. He wants more than anything to chuck them into the sea, but the men are watching.

"Smack them in the head, boy," Matty says. "It's kinder."

Matty clambers off the boat onto the quayside, strides over to where Gil crouches over the doomed fish. He takes up a stone, marked on one side with the traces of a fossilised fern, and whacks one, then the other. The gasping stops.

"You're a daft one," Matty says, pushing one hand roughly over Gil's scalp. Gil ducks, bundles the fish into his t-shirt, hurries off up the hill.

Morwenna is at the kitchen table on her laptop when he enters. She looks up as he places his t-shirt beside her, the smile dropping from her eyes as she sees his expression.

"Fish. From Uncle Matty," he says, and darts upstairs before she can do more than reach a hand towards the bundle.

He'd seen his uncle use a different dispatch method once before, reaching his fingers into the mackerel's mouth and shoving the head back sharply, breaking its neck. It had seemed so intrusive, so brutal that Gil had been unable to stop screaming. Matty was bemused.

"It's quick and painless," he'd said, lowering himself onto his haunches and trying to get Gil to meet his gaze.

Morwenna had made him promise he'd never do it in front of Gil again; had even given him the fern-stippled rock as an alternative. Gil sees Matty handling it occasionally with a strange tenderness in his eyes.

Matty has never married. He always claims that he's wed to the sea, but Gil notices the way he looks at Morwenna sometimes. He knows, too, that the 'mor' part of his mother's name is the Cornish word for sea. The duality of the thought hurts his head.

He leaves the house before dawn, pads down to the harbour, barefooted. The wind is restless, biting at his skin, murmuring things he can't catch enough to understand.

The moon is waxing, fatter than yesterday but still not halfway full. Clouds flurry across its glow, casting shadows over the waves. Gil strips off his t-shirt and shorts, shivers as the wind wraps around him. He climbs down the metal steps, slips into the water, allowing the chill to seep over him, into him. Become the blood in his veins. He sinks until his ears are submerged, then deeper still, seeking the hush beneath the surface.

He swims to the hull of Matty's boat, heaves himself on board, inhales. The air smells fierce; tastes bitter in his mouth. A storm is coming.

He thinks of the way Leonard said he had to be brave, how being hidden might be less than brave.

Closing his eyes against the moon's stare, Gil nods to himself.

He reaches into the bag at his throat and draws out a palmful of tiny shells. There are plenty – enough for him to defend the welfare of everyone.

But he thinks of his uncle, the man's ruddy face, the awkward hand that rubbed over his head earlier. Crouching low, he presses the shells into each whirl of rope, rowlock rim, winch and cleat. The rest he piles neatly on the deck, where Matty can't fail to see them.

Then he lowers his body into the truculent, trembling sea, and swims back to land. Up on the hill he can see his parents' house and the light that shines out from the kitchen window, and he wonders which one of them is waiting for him to return, safe.

Reeds and Curlews

THE SUSPENSION BRIDGE tries to catch us in its wires as we drive from Bristol to Wales, chasing storm clouds as we go. "It's a spider with a gazillion legs," Oli says, staring up through the sunroof.

I can't help but smile. In those words I hear the little boy he used to be, just last year or the year before. Not that twelve is so very close to full maturity, but the perils in his vicinity seem disturbingly adult.

The thirsty July ground is too hard-baked to let rain soak in. Puddles form, then lakes and rivers, gushing down hillsides to meet us. The deluge fills me with a kind of fierce delight. I feel we're amorphous – regressing to the amphibious beings we were in the womb.

"I was never a frog," Oli says, holding tight to the backpack cradled in his lap. One hand is closed in a fist, gripping something I can't see.

"No, but you were a wriggler," I say, my own hands fixed to the steering wheel as we aquaplane for a second, and then regain the road. "Hungry yet?"

He shakes his head, and I wonder if he's lying rather than risk enduring the hyper-lit ambush of a service station.

"Let's wait till we're there," he suggests.

I pop open the glove compartment so he can see the cereal bars inside. "Ok, but we have these if you get hungry beforehand."

From the corner of my eye I watch him stare at the bright wrappers, and then shake his head, some internal battle lost or won. "It'll make me need a drink. We don't have water, do we?"

"You could open the window and stick your tongue out," I joke, but he scowls.

"That water's dirty, dummy."

"Dummy!" I mask my dismay by pushing pretend anger into my voice. "Not nice, Oli."

He blinks at me for a beat, freckles dark against his pale cheeks. "Sorry, Mum."

"'s'ok. Look at the fields out there. Tell me when you see a sheep, or a zebra, or a ray of sunshine, yeah?"

He laughs, and I feel the tension in my chest dissipate.

We reach Laugharne just in time to grab a fish supper from the chippie. I lead the way across to the bench that sits below the castle. Rain has cleared, presenting a perfect green evening. The Taf Estuary shines in front of us, pinned at the edges, momentarily, by reeds and wading birds.

Oli looks at his sheaf of chips as if each one might contain a tiny grenade.

"If you don't start eating those, the gulls'll mob us," I say as lightly as I can manage.

He bares his teeth, and shoves two into his mouth, and another, making what should have been a pleasure into a chore. A pause, and then he stuffs in two more. I keep count, knowing he is doing the same. Prime numbers, divisible by themselves and one.

When we ball up the chip papers and chuck them in the bin, I feel the weight of my son's uneaten food.

We stroll up the hill to Dylan's writing shed, as we have done ever since Oli was tiny. He peers in at the space furnished and cluttered as if the poet's just stepped out for a moment; meandered down to the pub.

I stand a short distance behind Oli as he lays one palm flat against the shed's locked door. The other is still a fist. He knocks the item contained within it gently on the windowpane and I hear the impact of metal meeting glass.

"Dylan Thomas drank himself to death," he says suddenly, his voice sailing out over the estuary with the curlews.

I hold myself steady. "I know."

"I don't think he meant to do it," he says. "Do you?"

The tone is confrontational – almost an accusation.

I think of his friend, his best friend, the little boy I once knew as Mikey when Oli was still Oliver or Wriggler. The pair of them would bound around our garden like Labradors. Whenever I ventured into their territory to bring them snacks, Mikey would halt whatever game they were playing and gaze up at me as though I were a giant.

"He was ill, Oli. Dylan Thomas. Alcohol is as addictive as…" I hesitate, but push on through, determined not to wimp out. "…as any other drug."

Oli nods. "Mick didn't mean it either." He rocks the slim silver gas canister from one palm to another. A genie's bottle, once brimming with poisoned wishes.

I think of Oli rushing into the house, dragging me to my feet, blurred with shock. *Mick*, he'd cried again and again, *Mick's on the ground.*

I hadn't understood until he held out the empty nitrous oxide capsule, so I closed my fingers around its coldness. The call I made to emergency services was coherent, measured, my breathing stabilised by the prime numbers I counted to draw up the necessary words. It's the method I taught Oli to calm him out of asthma attacks when he was young, and has skated me over countless hillocks of stress.

Neither of us had known that laughing gas could kill. Deaths via the drug are rare, but not unheard of. I think of Mick on the ambulance gurney, as pale as milk. I imagine Oli inhaling the drug, his airways closing up.

But he's beside me, cheeks flushed from the exertion of the climb, perhaps with emotion.

No amount of numbers, or equations, will ease out whatever words could help now. Instead I tilt forward and rest one cheek against my son's back and feel the warmth flow between us, sense the beat of his pulse. He leans slightly into my touch, and I feel a dizzying thankfulness that he's the one who lived.

Fin

IT BEGAN AFTER their trip to the Azores. Toby had booked it as a celebration of their years together, complete with a voyage to look out for whales. Rachel glued on a smile and let Toby take her hand when he reached for it. She didn't know how to tell him it was over, but something in the skitter of his glance made her wonder if he'd already guessed. It was as though he no longer dared to fully see her, in case he mistakenly found himself staring at a truth he'd rather not face.

Of the numerous species those Atlantic waters attracted, it was the fin whales that deigned to make an appearance. While other tourists, including Toby, stood and snapped photos, lens to eye, Rachel sat back in her seat and drank the sight in. The slap of fin against the waves, the slide of an immense, narrow body swooning up then over and down into the depths. "Second largest mammal after the Blue Whale," their biologist tour guide commented. "These ones are behaving strangely. Normally they come up for air only, but these ones have risen, what, three, four times?"

Each time the pair rose, they came a little closer, and each time, Rachel felt herself singled out by their deep-set, knotted gaze.

Back home in Bristol, the sensation stayed with her – a movement like a shadow caught in the corner of her eye, the curve of a dive barely glimpsed, a large, sleek shape sliding through the periphery of her vision.

The echo of a sight.

She and Toby worked hard on settling into the house they'd barely moved into before flitting off on holiday. There were still boxes waiting to be unpacked, nails without pictures, rolled rugs standing sentinel in corners. Rachel found herself imagining the house without Toby, of the pleasing space his absence would create. It neatly matched the satisfaction of finding the perfect spot for each item, and of discarding others. A fresh start.

Then it began to rain. Toby hefted a box of boxes within boxes, and began the treacherous climb into the cellar.

He re-emerged moments later. "Flooded," he declared, grim-mouthed. "A foot of water, at least."

"Oh no!" Rachel exclaimed, her mind flickering suddenly with something close to joy. She resisted the urge to discard her shoes and socks there and then.

Toby had left the cellar door open. Each time Rachel passed its gaping maw, she felt its darkness sucking at the air that surrounded her. She waited until late that evening, when Toby was out playing badminton, then went to the top of the steep stairs, clicked on the light and peered down.

The water that had slunk in was well over a foot deep. More intriguingly, Rachel thought, it wasn't entirely still. Rather, it lapped the lowest steps, small waves heaving and breaking against the brick walls.

A smell wafted from the wet – a subtle, seaside reek of salt and fish. Rachel breathed in deeply and held the aroma within her, marrying it to the sight-echo shifting in her mind's eye. The two seemed to go together somehow.

She smiled inwardly, stepped back, and closed the door.

During the night the sense of movement, of some vast body silking through ocean depths, became increasingly pervasive. With Toby snoring beside her, she sat bolt upright in bed, momentarily concerned her lungs lacked the capacity to take her where she wanted to be.

With ankles and soles bare beneath her pyjamas, Rachel crept downstairs. This time she had no need to turn on the cellar light, as a stray moon seemed to have snuck inside to marinate the scene in silver.

The water was unfathomably deep – far deeper than the cavity of that subterranean room could hope to contain.

Rachel tiptoed to the very last step that raised its shoulders above sea level. A shiver danced through her as a wave trembled free and dashed itself to pieces against her skin.

At the rear of the cellar, where the moon shone least bright, a huge, slim shape broke through, curved over, and sank.

Rachel held her breath, seeing the fin glide up and out and under; the sly, tempting flick of a tail. She crouched down, dipping in her fingers, and then one hand until the icy water had enveloped her palm up to her wrist. As if responding to her touch, the fin whale turned, looped twice and surfaced just beyond her reach. Its gaze met hers and she smiled with the shock of recognition, with the bedazzlement of seeing and being seen.

Blossoming Almond Tree

WE TRAVELLED TO Amsterdam as a celebration the year you turned eighteen. Mam wasn't thrilled but I promised her we'd visit too many museums to keep straight in our brains, and that I'd make sure you did nothing more than look at the other options on offer.

I planned to keep at least half that promise.

You'd been quieter than usual in the run up to your exams, only your wordless humming occasionally breaking the silence of several days.

I knew Mam was worried about you. I dug into that anxiety and assured her that seeing a bit of culture would do you good, especially with me, your big sister, to watch over you. She couldn't argue with that.

The journey to Bristol airport took longer and cost more than the flight to Schiphol.

Somehow, we managed to hit a heat wave that slowed the city to a gentle saunter. We strolled around gawping at the canal houses with their gabled façades, and then went and sat on the National Monument in Dam Square eating cones of chips strung with mayonnaise.

I was intrigued by the smoothness of the travertine stone riddled with tiny cavities – like the marks left by miniature artillery fire. "Maybe these are from when the city was occupied, Davey," I suggested, running my fingers over the pitted stone.

You shook your head; gaze fixed on a posse of women on a hen do who were already half-cut and wobbling on rented bikes. "I read about this. They built it in 1956, as a memorial to the dead of World War II."

"Then why the holes?"

"Could be weather damage." You shrugged. "Travertine's a form of limestone, Elise – a sedimentary rock."

As if that would clarify anything for me.

You didn't shift your attention from the bride, her cloud of veil patched with lipstick and fraying at the edges.

The girls in windows enthralled you too; I watched you watching them with a sort of delighted disquiet in your eyes. Even at 9.30am on a Sunday, when the only other businesses open were churches, the girls worked, yawning as they smiled and beckoned.

"Do you think they're exploited?" you asked. "They remind me of caged pigeons – in better shape than the ones on the street, but do you think they're happy?"

I shrugged, unsure why you expected me to be able to answer that when I couldn't guess whether you, my own brother, were happy.

Amsterdam's girls were available in a dazzling array of nationalities: every shape, size, race and persuasion – options for any mood and taste, just like the weed.

I wasn't sure I wanted to smoke while we were there – I didn't always relish the fog it brought down – but I saw your expression twitch as we passed the cafés and didn't want you thinking me old and fuddy-duddy already at twenty-three. We chose a café where the windows were painted with portraits of Bob Marley and a world-weary lioness lipping a spliff.

Time grew sticky; heavy. Your increasingly disjointed comments came at me as though underwater. I felt moved to laugh even when I wasn't sure I'd understood what you'd said.

We sat and jabbered; drizzle began to mist over the canals. It reminded me of how it rains at Lake Glas, that place where we spent so much of our childhood, like it rains nowhere else – sky and water turned upside down.

"Droplets plummet from clouds to create circles that spread outwards like… Like rumours heard and misconstrued," I rhapsodised as you listened, entranced. "Each one's a tiny magic trick – now you see it, now you don't. How could something so separate, so complex, so completely merge with the whole? In the moments before it collides, each one's an individual entity with a future of infinite possibilities." I hesitated, lowering my voice intentionally so you had to crane in to listen. "Then it meets the lake, meets its fate, meets, in a sense, its maker. And is gone."

"Sounds well lush," you breathed. "You know, that's what I think happens when we die – we become part of everything. Life after life after life after death."

You'd been pleased with that hypothesis, I thought.

Afterwards, still thickened by dope, we took a boat ride along canals that glistened with a viscous quality – something that had been simmered and left to cool.

I found myself transfixed by the undersides of bridges – they resemble entrances to a secret underworld – some had narrow steps leading down from the light-filled terra firma above. Every stretch of wood or rise of stone or brick was laced with a green so bright I thought I could taste it in the air.

It made me think of something, some fairytale or myth, but my memories had grown too slippery to capture.

You were more interested in the houseboats anyway, crying out now and then: "We could live there, Elise – that one's perfect."

I managed to dredge my gaze from the bridges and found you pointing to a teal-green houseboat that resembled an upturned shoebox, with neat, square windows and a ludicrous a white picket fence at the front.

"We're too tall to live there," I countered. "There's not room to swing a cat, and we'd need a cat." It was true, every shop and home in Amsterdam had its own feline security guard, each doing its bit to curtail the city's rodent population.

"That's what I could do with," you said so softly I wasn't sure whether you'd spoken to yourself or me. "A cat for my mind, to swat away the creeping thoughts I didn't invite in."

Something about the tension in your face reminded me of visiting your school one spring day when my own was closed for some administrative reason, and yours was not.

I ambled over to see if my old teachers would be astonished by how transformed I was: a teenager, compared to the child they'd known.

The familiar shrieks of children letting loose a build-up of energy crackled around me.

I wondered if I might catch a glimpse of you playing with your mates, and glanced across the playground. A haze of scaffolding glinted over the building.

There, I thought to myself sanguinely, proof that nothing stays the same.

I couldn't see you in the jostling mass; thought nothing of it, and meant to go on.

I've never been sure what caught my attention at that point. Perhaps I caught your eight-year-old shape in the corner of my eye and filled in the rest.

You were high up, unnaturally high, a silhouetted form against the sharpness of the April sky.

The scaffolding shone hard and metallic – half cliff, half cage.

That was enough. I erupted into the playground – it was easy to do in those pre-security days – and hurtled towards the crowd gathered beneath where you hung. The children were laughing and catcalling, but hushed each other when I joined them.

I wanted to yell out, to raise my voice in mimicry of Bebby's sternest tones and demand you come down.

Something about the way you clung there, unmoving, made me hold in my shout, afraid to startle you.

"What happened?" I asked the congregated kids. "Why's he up there?"

Most of them ignored me, fixated on your figure above as though expecting some grand metamorphosis.

Did they think you were about to take flight?

"What *happened*?" I asked louder, and a stocky blond lad shrugged.

"Who knows? That's Crazy Davey, int it? He does all sorts."

"All sorts?" I resisted the urge to grab the boy by his jacket. "All sorts of what?"

The boy shrugged again, lips clamping together.

I lowered myself so we were eye to eye and hissed: "Did someone scare him into climbing the scaffolding? Did someone chase him up there, you little scrotum?"

The boy started snivelling. "I'll tell a teacher on you!"

"Will you now?" I yelled, as he shoved his way out of the throng and flailed into a run. "And while you're squawking to the teachers about me calling you a *scrotum*..." I sang out the word loud enough to send an awed hush through my audience. "...do send one over this way."

A ripple spread around me – a flare of shock shot through with the wobbly joy of a bit of drama.

No adolescent had ever infiltrated their school to yell obscenities before.

You turned slightly so the light illuminated your profile. I could see that though tear-streaked, you didn't look afraid.

"Davey." I carefully pinched the panic from my voice. "What're you doing? Come down, won't you?"

You saw me and frowned, then smiled a welcome. "Elise!"

The scaffolding creaked as wind whistled through it.

I imagined I saw the structure rock.

I wrapped my fingers around the closest metal tube. It felt as cold, and as slippery as ice. Your hands must have been nearly numb. However serene you seemed, there was no way you'd chosen to climb up.

I glowered at the spectators. "Why don't you lot go and play? Go on, now, get lost."

"You can't tell us what to do – you're not an adult," squawked one.

"Yeah, but I'm thirteen, much closer to being one than you are, and closer than you'll ever be if you don't fuck off."

They scattered across the playground.

Neck craned backwards, I caught the way your eyes flickered from the surrounding views to the space opening around the base of the scaffolding.

'I've got to go in a minute," I said.

"Can I come with you?" you asked.

More than anything, I wanted to promise yes, to vow that if you climbed down right now you could do anything you wanted.

But I knew you'd remember the lie. I could feel myself on the brink of pleading, and had to smother the pitch rising through me.

"I don't think so," I said at last, as calmly as I could manage. "But I'm right here, and I want to see you properly, before I leave."

You blinked at me, immobile.

"Did you hear what I called that boy? What's his name? With the blond hair and round face like a football."

I heard a sound escape you, a sort of laugh. In a wheeze, you gasped: "Scrotum."

"What's that, Davey? Speak up, I don't think I heard you."

"Scrotum!" you bellowed, so sudden and loud that a line of pigeons burst from the school building roof into the air, as if offended.

I giggled. "Too right! We've been doing human reproduction at school. If you come down now I'll tell you all the bad words you'll ever need."

"Like what?" you asked, and I could see you grinning.

"Like…" I thought fast, picturing the page in my biology book. "Like *uterus*."

"Uterus," you echoed, then bawled: "Uterus!"

I laughed with you. "Come down and I'll tell you another."

I didn't expect it to work; swearing wasn't really your thing. But I think you genuinely wanted to be at ground level.

All I was doing was giving you an excuse to surrender the high ground you'd cornered yourself into.

I watched you move one hand, dangle one foot, and begin to make your way down the structure.

I didn't make the tiniest sound, barely inhaled, until you stood beside me.

We were both panting. You turned and smiled at me, and I enveloped you in a fierce cwtch. "If you ever, *ever*, do anything like that again, I'll hike up and shove you off myself. You hear me?"

Your reply was smothered by the fabric of my coat.

A teacher appeared at last, a harassed-looking man I didn't know. His straggling goatee suggested he'd tried, and failed, to grow a full beard.

The blond, football-faced boy trailed after him.

I could taste the outrage in my throat. "Where were you?" I demanded. "Where were you when my brother needed you?"

The anger fell from the man's expression, replaced by alarm.

I held myself tall and haughty until I'd said goodbye to you and stalked off the school grounds.

I never did uncover what fear or humiliation had driven you to scale the scaffolding.

I tried asking, but when you skidded past the question, eyes flickering blue, relief burned under my skin.

I told myself that the important thing was that you'd got down in one piece. Believed it, too, for many years.

"Everyone has those thoughts," I said after a moment, on that boat traversing Amsterdam's waterways. "You just have to find a way to live with them. It's why some people pray, and others overeat."

"And you draw," you murmured, catching me off-guard.

My pulse twitched. Until then I hadn't suspected anyone else knew about my bordering-on-obsessive doodling.

You smiled sheepishly, and reached into your pocket, bringing out a crumpled napkin. You turned it over and flattened it out, revealing a sketch I'd discarded in Bristol airport a day and a half earlier. This one was patterned with spirals and double-helixes, as well as sketches of the wildlife we'd seen at Lake Glas – speckled frogs, mud snails, mayfly larva and a shrew, drowned, with tiny starry hands like panicked stars.

"I've been collecting them," you confessed, "for years."

"Oh," I said, because I didn't know what else to say.

In truth, what I wanted, more than anything, in that instant, was to shove you into the nearest strip of canal, perhaps see you strike your skull hard on the way down.

"You can't say they were private, when you left them there for anyone to find," you added hurriedly, suddenly defensive.

Not anyone that knows me, I thought, not the one person in the world most likely to be able to connect those scraps and make sense of them.

The moment the boat pulled in at the next jetty, I pushed my way through a mess of mitchers onto the embankment, almost stepping into the path of a trio of cyclists. Their shouts startled me into darting to the side. I carried on darting, then broke into a run and raced down the cobbled paths.

I felt my flash had been flayed by the violation of you examining something I'd thought hidden. My skin flapped behind me – my own version of the bride's torn veil.

You caught up with me in a courtyard, outside a shop selling brass casts of cloven hooves and innumerable glass eyes.

"Elise." You rested your chin on my shoulder. "Don't be tamping."

"I'm not." I cupped your scalp, resting my cheek against your locks. "It's only... you're the first to see them properly."

To see me.

"Well, who better that than me?" you asked, blinking up at me in such surety of my forgiveness that I could only laugh and cuff your curls.

The next day, our last in the city, we visited The Van Gogh Museum and spent an age standing in front of his painting of almond branches blooming. There was a sweetness to discovering how *Blossoming Almond Tree* came to be, how the artist been confined to a mental hospital at the time, and created it to mark the birth of his brother's first child.

I savoured the serenity in that – a reminder that however bleak things seem, the generosity of finding gladness in a sibling's good fortune could strip away the clouds.

"Look, Davey," I said as we studied at his masterpiece. "The notice says he chose to paint the almond tree because it flowers as early as February, heralding the hope of spring to follow winter."

I stopped talking then, already wary of glorifying a man who'd taken his own life within months of painting a scene of such joy.

*

On the plane journey home, I let you have the window seat, wanting to amend for my reaction to you seeing my drawings. You sat there, half inclined towards the sky, sunlight playing over your features.

I took out the stub of my boarding pass, and on the back of it I drew a quick biro sketch of you, my exquisite brother.

"Here," I said, and I slid it onto the tray table in front of you, my mind jumping like a box full of frogs.

Merrow Cave

IT'S CARVED INTO the side of the rock – a face tilted to one side, hair streaming behind. The jaw is angular and strong, the whole thing larger than life.

Running his hands over the smooth stone of the cheeks and nose, Callum senses it again, that feeling of someone behind him, watching. He lets his arms drop to his sides and turns, slowly, gazing into the darkness at the rear of the cave. The shadows are so deep he feels blind for a moment, but then there's something, a movement of some sort, and the thin light crawling in from the entrance snags on something back there.

"Hello?" he calls, and his voice bleeds back to him, causing him to shudder with self-consciousness. He wants to run outside into the sunshine, but as the last echoes ebb away, he hears something very like a cough being stifled. Whatever it is in the darkness, it sounds unwell.

"Callum, come on, we're having the picnic now!" His Auntie Reen is at the entrance, smiling at him.

He can guess the kinds of things that picnic basket holds, and his stomach clenches. "I'm not hungry."

"Not hungry? 'course you are! Growing lad saying he's not hungry?" She tuts, disbelief sharp in her voice.

He follows her onto the beach, blinks in the sunlight. Grumph is sitting on a folding chair in front of a chequered blanket, hands folded over his sagging stomach, staring out to sea.

"Ah, there you are, Callum. Hungry, is it? Reen's made, what was it? Ham sandwiches and things."

The sandwiches are exactly that, ham without a slither of anything else to makes the thick dry bread go down easier. The 'things' turn out to be not quite successfully hard-boiled eggs, the whites quivering unappetisingly inside the shells, and little pies made from rubbery pastry that Callum prods with one finger then discreetly sets aside. He doesn't dare ask what kind of pies they are. The egg he tips from its shell onto the sand where it sits in a slippery yellow-centred puddle.

"Ah, this is the stuff," says Grumph. "Sea air, a picnic, a few seals out there, I reckon, to boot! Something to write home to your ma about, eh?"

"Seals, Grumph?" he asks, gnawing on a corner of sandwich.

"Out there, boy, beyond the breakers. Can see 'em now and again, a shiny nose bobbing up."

Callum shields his eyes with one hand, but can't be sure what's driftwood, what's shadow and what might, just might, be a seal. "Saw one in the cave, I think," he says instead.

"Cave, which cave?"

"The one with the carving in it, of the face," Callum says.

"He's been in the Merrow Cave, Da."

The old man goes still and silent for a moment, eyes clouding over, then he nods. "If you're not going to eat that pie, why not leave it at the cave entrance then, eh? She might fancy it."

"Who, Grumph? The seal?"

But his grandfather doesn't answer, seemingly absorbed in watching the waves breaking against themselves.

*

Callum has been on the island for three days now, and already time is taking on a vague, shifting quality that follows the tides. If it wasn't for the drift in light, he isn't sure he'd know how much time had passed. He is growing accustomed to the half-darkness that makes up so much of his waking hours.

He misses home; misses his parents and his friends. There are no other kids here to play footie with or race him up and down the shore. His aunt and grandfather have no neighbours, only gulls that ride the air currents like windsurfers taken to the sky. They run along the wet sand at the edge of the sea, pursuing the yellow-shelled crabs that skitter there.

Callum tries to imagine his ma growing up here with Reen and Grumph, chasing the wind and poking around in rock pools as he does, but when he pictures her he can only see her lying frail and narrow in bed as she had been when he left.

He thinks that the word for what she has, emphysema, echoes with how far she seems to be from him now. His dad had talked it through with him, explained how the air sacs in her lungs were withered away.

"What made it happen?" he'd asked, rubbing the side of his cheek against the blanket his mother slept under. The room smelled strongly of lavender that barely masked a thicker, heavier odour that lay beneath.

His dad looked away, then back, and said: "I made her leave the sea."

Callum sees Reen each morning emerging from the waves, translucent and gleaming. "You joinin' me tomorrow," she asks each time, and each time he grins, embarrassed, and shakes his head.

"Too cold for you, is it?" she asks, and he lets her accept his silence as agreement. He doesn't want to admit that, like his father, he doesn't know how to swim.

Callum doesn't remember visiting the island before, but now he sees it in its winter desolation, he can't imagine his mother minding too much about leaving with his dad. The few stunted trees are bent and shivering, skinny branches curling at the air like fingers grasping sheets. Inside the shuttered house, draughts wheeze through every crack and pepper his skin with goosebumps even when he's in bed. Everything creaks with the relentless shushing sound of the sea.

"How d'you hear yourself think here?" he asks Auntie Reen. "It's so noisy!"

"Noisy?" She stares at him, then smiles. "I've lived here all my life, pet. Whatever you hear is just background to me. I don't notice it any more than you do the sounds of your own body."

Which intrigues him so much that he spends a good while trying to identify whatever murmurs his body might make, and soon finds he can hear it, if he concentrates: beneath the whispering sea and the ticking clocks and the endless wind there's a sort of hum deep inside him, like a distant, comforting rumble of underground trains.

He tries to listen to it when he wakes from a nightmare, tries to latch onto that sense of reassurance, but isn't sure he can make it out over the groans of the house around him. The wind seems wilder without the light of day; he's sure it's trying to shove the house right onto the beach.

Then he thinks he feels the tiny hairs in his ear canal stiffen, catching hold of a quick, wet lapping sound like a dog at a pail of water. He freezes, yes, there it is, but it isn't oozing from his own saturated depths.

He slips out of bed and creeps to the window, trying to focus on the heaving sea in the blackness beyond. He blinks, once, twice, and sees something moving at the foot of the shallow cliff the house sits against. Something crouching low and licking at the damp sand he poured his mess of unset egg onto.

Trembling, he unbolts the window, gives it a little push. At once the wind grasps it, slams it wide open against the wall of the house.

The creature below stares up, eyes large in its oval face, then it slinks away, retreating towards the Merrow Cave.

Morning comes and with it a breakfast of gristly pork sausages and hard potato cakes. Grumph chews with relish, as though his daughter's cooking is the best in the world. Maybe, Callum thinks, he hasn't tasted anything else, not in decades anyway. No one speaks of the grandmother who must have lived here at some time, must have existed in order for his ma, and therefore him, to exist now.

There's a photo on his grandfather's bedside table that might be of her: a woman half silhouetted against the sun, half turned to the sea. The photo's colours must have warped with age; her long hair looks almost green, her skin paler than it ought to.

Reen walks in as he's staring at it. "All right, Callum? What you up to?"

"Is that my gran?" he asks and sees her eyes flicker.

"Callum, pet," she says, hesitant. "What's your ma told you about our family, then? She told you about what we are?"

He shakes his head, wondering what she can mean.

"Ma's got emfarseemer," he says, pronouncing the word with care. He thinks of what his dad told him. "Is it because she lives so far from the sea?"

Reen says sadly: "Perhaps."

He watches her eyes dart to another photo – this one hanging from the paisley wallpaper by the door. It shows two girls in matching swimming costumes with frills at the shoulders. They're laughing and posing. He thinks the shorter, red-haired one might be his mum; the more muscular dark-haired one Reen. They both have the same ghostly, freckled skin, the same slightly beaked nose, as he does.

Later that day he watches his aunt leave the house with the picnic basket. Grumph is snoozing in his armchair, lips vibrating with each outward breath.

The sky outside is as pink-tinged as undercooked meat. Callum slips out of the back door and follows at a distance, sees her step into the shadows of the Merrow Cave. He skulks in after her, halts just inside the entrance, below the carving of the serene face.

"All right, Ma?" he hears his aunt say. "Got some potato cakes here. You hungry?"

He hears an odd whistling noise in return, akin to the sound of wind in the cracks of the house. He edges closer, heart pounding, his breath coming in gasps. The creature is curled up in a pool at the far end, raising its head as if smelling the air. Its scalp is covered with sparse strands of hair, like seaweed over a smooth domed rock. As he stares, open-mouthed, it turns towards him and emits a long, shrill shriek.

Callum doesn't stop running until he's in the bedroom, the door closed at his back. He crouches down, hugging his knees and wishing he were at home, with his ma.

The knock comes moments later, as he knew it would. "Callum, pet? Let me in, will you?" His aunt's voice sounds anxious, and more than a bit like his ma's. It calms him enough that he shuffles away from the door till he's pressed against the bed, draughts weaving in through every nook in the room.

Reen comes and sits beside him, holds out her hands for him to see. The backs of them are rougher than he'd noticed, starred with tiny scales that remind him of the marks running down his ma's spine, that his dad once told him were scars from a boating accident. That was one of the excuses his dad gave for not letting him learn to swim. "The ocean's dangerous. If you can swim, you'll want to go in the water, and anything could happen." It doesn't sound so daunting now, more enticing than frightening.

"Your grumph met your grandma on that shore out there," Auntie Reen says slowly. "She invited him to swim with her and that was it, he could never leave."

Callum thinks about that, about how with his parents it was the other way round: his dad invited his mum to join him on the mainland, and she never came home.

"The carving in the Merrow Cave, your grumph did that so she could see his love for her. But she's old now, and she's forgetting him; forgetting your mother and I ever existed." She pauses, sighs. "She can't find the words he taught her now. What you heard, that's how they communicate. But Da can't understand it, and I think she's forgettin' how to understand him too."

"She's not well. I heard her coughing."

"She's old, pet, years older than your grumph. Don't reckon she's got long."

He takes a breath, hearing his thoughts beneath the sounds of the sea and the wind. "Ma might not have long either, not if she's stays over there all that way from the sea."

Reen glances at him and he sees her throat move as she swallows. For a moment she's just like the face carved into the rock in the cave. "I reckon your gran misses her, even if she is losing her memories. She and your ma always had a special bond."

Callum touches her hand, feels the smooth hardness of the scales studding her skin. "We should ring my dad, tell him to bring her home, so they can see each other. And Grumph would like that too, wouldn't he?"

He doesn't add the other part of what he's thinking, that he yearns to see his ma more than anything. And that if there's the tiniest possibility bringing her to the sea could save her, he wants to take that chance.

*

They make the phone call after tea. Grumph listens in, huffing as Callum talks to his father. "Please bring her," Callum begs.

"Ah, Cal, she's not well enough to travel. You know that."

Callum hesitates, trying to hear if she's there in the background. The connection crackles faintly. "Ask her, Dad, please, ask if she wants to see us."

"Callum!" His dad sounds upset. "It's just not going to happen."

Grumph takes the receiver from Callum and barks into it like an old seal: "Now, you listen here, the boy wants to see his ma. I'm the fool who let you take her from us. Now you be the fool wise enough to bring her back, eh?"

Callum hears his father exclaiming on the other end, then growing quieter until Grumph hangs up crossly.

"Now what'll we do?" Callum asks, dread cold inside him.

"Now we wait," the old man says, then mutters, "Sure, we have all the time in the world."

The phone rings just as he's about to get into bed. Reen shouts to him and he runs downstairs in his pajamas, feeling draughts pushing at him from every corner of the house.

"Callum?" his dad says, his voice throaty with wonder. "I asked her like you said. She opened her eyes. I haven't seen her do that in days. She looked right at me." He gasps like he can't quite believe what he's about to say. "We're coming, son. We'll be with you in two days."

Callum shudders with the suddenness of the joy in his chest. "Dad!" He can't speak for a moment, then thinks of the tea he struggled through that evening – the clammy quiche and oddly gritty potato salad. "Dad, bring some frozen pizzas, won't you? Give Reen and Grumph a taste of our home."

*

Dawn is barely touching the horizon when Callum races down the beach. He's almost as speedy as the seagulls after lemon-shelled, scuttling crabs, and dashes straight into the silver-tipped waves where he halts in the shallows, letting the icy tide drag at his ankles.

The air smells salty and cold and green. He breathes it in as deep as he can, filling his lungs.

Before long Reen appears, powerful arms slicing through the water towards where he stands.

"You joining me tomorrow?" she asks as she nears him.

"I'd like to join you now," he says shyly, a hotness rising in his cheeks. "If you'll teach me."

Reen cups her scale-backed hands to his cheeks, smiling. Then she throws back her head and screeches into the wind.

Far out beyond the breakers, Callum thinks he hears an answering shriek, welcoming him to the sea.

Milk and Other Lies

ONE DAY THE river runs with milk. I watch as hollow-eyed mothers bring infants to the shallows. They pour the clouded liquid, scooped palm by palm, into their babies' gaping mouths.

The next day I wake to the sound of children's laughter. I step outside, smelling a cloying sweetness in the air. The river has been gilded overnight, shining with butterscotch. Children hurtle in, barefoot – hungry for its sweet promises.

"Does it fill you up?" I ask a boy the age my son would have been. His lips are caked white with sugar flakes. The flecks shift as he grins, cracking apart like insects' latticed wings.

The following morning, the river brims with broth, its aroma inviting in the old, the infirm – anyone in need of a nurturing feed. It also draws the fat flesh-feasting flies that more often signal the passing of some old grandmother or goat.

I wait until all have drunk their fill, pushing down my own unease.

"I wish for water," I say aloud, and with a twitch the river turns as clear as the sky. In its rippled mirror I see our famine-swollen, stick-limbed bodies.

But today the water is cool. It dances with sunlight. It quenches my thirst and I wade in.

Edge of the Sand

THE TIDE HAS just begun to turn. Arianne walks along the edge of the sand, collecting seagull feathers one by one. They're white, the feathers, and dappled with grey, mirroring the clouds overhead.

Her meandering route carries her to the narrow stairs that lead to her childhood home. Deepening shadows cast a chill over clumps of delicate purple flowers that sprout from the cracks between rocks. Her dad would have known what they were named. He always knew details like that – it was he who first got her interested in insects and other invertebrates when she was barely more than a dot herself.

The back door is sticky, its wood swollen by spring rain. She forces it open and steps into the stillness and stands motionless for a moment, feeling the thrum of her heart.

"Ari?"

"Yes, Mum!" She fans out the seagull feathers on the hall table.

A sharp reek scratches at her throat as she enters the room where Odessa sits in the light streaming through the window. The dress her mother wears is shapeless, but shiny. It makes her look like an iridescent beetle – a rose chafer, perhaps, Arianne thinks.

"What's that smell, Mum?"

"Smell, what smell?" Odessa's gaze flickers back to the window, keeping watch on the sky.

Arianne looks at Odessa properly, noticing the lank hair, lacklustre skin. Something's not right. "Mum, haven't you been washing?"

"Shower's broken." Odessa hesitates, eyes darting. "Taps too. Water's freezing cold. Enough to make your tits blue."

"Mum!"

Arianne goes into the kitchen and turns on a tap. She waits, but the flow doesn't warm. "Something wrong with the boiler," she shouts to her mum. "I'll get Rich Ramsgate to come, yeah? He might have to get some lads in."

"I don't want strangers here," Odessa protests. "You said there's a smell."

"I'll boil up some water after I've put the tea on. You can have a splash bath. That's what Dad called it, isn't it? When we went camping? Freshen you up."

"They'll want me to come to the door."

"I'll give Rich a key, explain they're not to bother you. That'll be ok, won't it?"

"Why can't you try fixing it?" There's a squeak of panic to Odessa's voice. "Or ask your brother?"

"I haven't got a clue about that kind of thing, Mum." She presses down her irritation, ashamed by it, and tries to soften her tone. "Glyn's busy with the wedding, you know that." She pictures her little brother aged six or so, his gap-toothed grin, and sand, always sand, among the roots of his hair.

"Oh yes, the wedding."

Arianne ducks back into the living room and sees Odessa worrying her bottom lip with her teeth. She kneels down in front of her.

"Just a month till the big day." She warms the arthritic hands between her palms and then turns her attention to her mum's feet, giving them a good rub too. "I found a hat shop in town, a milliner's. Didn't know those places still existed. Want to come with me on the weekend? We could get you something special – proper mother-of-the-groom stuff."

"Oh no. No, I don't think so." Odessa turns back to the windowpane, resolute.

Arianne exhales, head bowed, and stands up, stamping the tingles from her lower limbs. "Ok, Mum. What d'you want for tea?"

*

The man comes, takes a long look at the boiler, then goes away, comes back with more men. They're laden with scaffolding to put up in front of her window – metal rods interfering with her view of the sky. In and out all morning, strutting on wooden planks like they think it's a stage.

Scattering her thoughts like clouds, birds, hailstones. Keeping the blue tits at bay.

"Should be right as rain now, Odessa," says Rich, who's no older than Glyn and ought really to call her Mrs Dawn, not Odessa.

She remembers waking to the sound of drizzle on camping trips when the children were no more than eight and ten, opening her eyes to see it weighing down the fabric above her – swollen as an egg yolk. Clive telling her to leave it alone, urging her to stay tucked up in his arms, but her unable to resist, reaching out, bumping it with her finger. No disaster followed, just a bit of wet, giggles, the love in his voice as he told her off.

If he were here now, there'd be no scaffolding, and she'd be up and out of the house with him to walk along the lick of waves, happy to let them lap her bare toes even if they turned her blue.

It seems strange that the cold once held no dread for her, that she could run against the wind and feel invigorated.

She knows she needs to wash, but fear steals over her as she stands in the bathroom doorway, feeling the ache of her calves, her ankles. *Silly*, she chides herself, trying to use Clive's voice in her head. *What harm can a bit of raw water do a strapping lass?* Not that he'd ever called her strapping. Not that she'd been anywhere near as big when he was alive. She feels her body is turning back into a baby's, muscles and bones slowly slipping to milk-fat.

Not statuesque as she'd once been, when she was happy to be seen by him, striding naked from the water – nipples large and alert with the chill.

"You're magnificent." Clive fell to his knees before her, as though awe-struck. She'd bit back embarrassed laughter, but felt the love in his embrace.

She hadn't known then that she'd get old and swollen and all but immobile. Hadn't guessed that sadness could make her heavy-limbed – that the very air would have a tide that pushed against her.

Clive had relished the way the cold raised her skin into miniscule bumps. "I can see where the breeze is nibbling you," he'd murmur, taking the flesh of her arm between his lips.

She grits her teeth, twists the shower on. The water that comes shines in the bulb's light. When the flow exhales steam, she pictures Clive standing in its deluge, hair slicked to wood grain against his body, beckoning her in.

*

The hat shop reminds Arianne of the butterfly house at the zoo – gauzy wings in various stages of preparation heaped here and there: concave, convex. She feels a moment's dizziness as she steps in from the cool arcade beyond. It's the same sensation she imagines her mum feels when contemplating venturing out.

"Can I help you?"

A petite dark-haired woman unfurls from a corner. She tilts the enquiring curve of her face towards Arianne.

Arianne blinks. She holds out her plastic bag of pilfered seagull feathers – the most beautiful, least tainted, she has found. "I wondered if you could…"

The woman's eyes are sharp points of light. Her hands remain by her sides, though she leans forward slightly, glancing at the shards of white and stippled grey.

"Could you make these into a hat for me?" Arianne asks.

The woman smiles, shakes her head. "No, but I may be able to teach you to."

The first step is to clean the feathers by rinsing them in tepid water, patting them dry, then placing them in the freezer overnight "just in case."

Arianne doesn't ask *in case of what?*

Next comes the shaping. "Here," says the milliner, passing Arianne the flat, crisp sheets of shadowy fabric. "This is Sinamay, made from banana plant fibres. Layer it up until you have the opacity you desire. Three is a good number."

She shows Arianne how to use steam to mould it over a wooden block, pulling it tight and securing it with pins. Now it resembles a stiff grey bloom, or a cloud atop a saucer.

The feathers, they're the most important part, Arianne thinks, taking care as she uses a blade to slice one side of the barb and the silky tendrils from the shaft before curling each tip like a ribbon. Others she shortens but leaves mostly intact, before gluing and sewing them to scraps of felt. The final stage is attaching them to the naked hat, transforming it into a flourish of salt-spray from the sea.

*

They used to lie on their backs in the sand; her head on his chest, watching the seagulls rise and fall. Riding the updrafts, sailing down with the cooler air. It didn't look turbulent, she thought, but peaceful – like giving your body to the waves.

That was Clive's phrase, for when the peaks and troughs were white-frilled and foaming, and he'd race in, eager. She'd hang back so she could see the sinews in his torso, his buttocks, the strength of his thighs and calves; experience the same shock of desire that emptied her lungs when they first met.

And then she'd follow. Usually.

She can't be certain now what kept her on shore, beachcombing while he inhaled the tide. The children were almost grown, most likely off with friends. Something had made her pause – a tangle of bright rope or a few shards of silk-fogged sea glass.

The hat Arianne has brought her is silvery. Gull's wings curl out and back, undecided about whether to ride thermals or swoop downwards.

Odessa runs her fingers over the feathers, and sways with the urge to crush them flat. She thinks of Arianne, the pleading in her eyes as she placed the box before her.

"For Glyn's wedding, Mum. So you can stand in front of everyone and not be scared." Arianne's voice caught on the words, brittle with hope.

It's a thing of beauty, that hat.

The machine beside her beeps again. She'd listened to Glyn's voice, hand hovering over the receiver before dropping to her lap. "Mum, it's me," he'd said. "Just checking in. You will be at the wedding, won't you?"

Clive would have wanted her to go along. Wouldn't be able to understand this fright of the cold, the wet, the very air.

After she lost him, clouds seeped inside the house, laying her out flat beneath their sodden weight. She'd barely been able to hear Ari and Glyn; as if they were on the other side of a window, out in the rain.

This hat, though, looks lighter than clouds, brighter than air. It has a sheen to it that makes her need to touch it, as she did the canvas of the tent. She pushes her fingertips against the fabric and feels it give; bounce back.

Odessa lifts the hat out of the box and holds it before her. The feathers tremble in a way that's reassuring. She raises her arms, placing the hat on her head. It sits there expectantly and she feels a faint tremor of excitement run through her.

Breath quickening, Odessa steps forwards and opens the window wide, letting the noises of the day in. Sounds whirl about her like the blue tits that have returned, unfazed by the scaffolding.

She fastens the window again, hearing Clive's voice in her head. *There, what was so bad about that?*

"Nothing," she whispers, "Nothing at all."

What Rises

I STIRRED AS I heard the river move beneath the crops, its murmurs rejoicing. My brothers lay intertwined beside me. "Fam's leaving," I whispered, and their eyes snapped open. We crept outside, leaving Dad asleep. We'd known this day would come, even before he struck her for the third time.

What rises from water can't live on land forever.

Outside, our mother was already a distant glimmer, her milk-white cattle streaming behind. We rushed after her, silenced by the dawn and the river and the intentness with which she strode.

At the lake's edge she turned, her fist-blackened eyes like shadows.

"Fam!" cried the youngest of us, Brychan, unable to keep his fear inside. "Fam, take me too."

He ran to her and we saw her place her water-cold fingers on his half-human cheeks.

"You stay here, son, you and your brothers. You stay here and tend to the people of the soil."

My elder brother Mab and I took our sobbing sibling between us, each with an arm over his shoulder. We thought comfort into him, and strength, performing our first act of healing.

Our mother waded into the water. Her cornflower-eyed, ash-freckled herd trailed in her wake, losing themselves to ripples and reflections of clouds.

*

She called me son, but I was always a daughter. She saw how the men of the soil behaved and feared for my future. She named me Eillian, meaning moment in time, and a name that does as well for a boy as a girl. She dressed me as she did my brothers, and gave me the same freedoms, so my actions were as rough and voice as loud as theirs.

People believe what their eyes tell them, and no one could have guessed I betrayed expectations beneath my clothes.

I was the middle child, and far from the most delicate of us three. In the hours after our mother left, our younger brother took a fever, and it was my elder brother Mab and I who cared for him with heat and herbs and the uncommon energy within us.

When our mother had wed our father she promised to leave if he raised a hand to her three times. We knew he'd slapped her, but we didn't know why. Local gossips said he raised his hand when she cried at a wedding, when she refused to attend a baptism and when she laughed during a funeral. But those seemed little more than myth, and we knew not what to trust.

It didn't help that our father never uttered a word once he'd lost his wife. In the evenings, he sat by the hearth and I watched his hands winding around each other, each palm pitying each fist.

Mab was the first of his offspring to change, growing suddenly taller, jaw roughened with hair. He showed Brychan and me the fur sprouting around his penis. "I'm as much beast now as man," he boasted. His voice became a raven, hacking and screeching in rhythm with the wind.

By rights I should have been next, but Brychan followed after, his pied cheeks losing their childish curve as his shoulders broadened and his voice mimicked a crow's.

My voice remained a sparrow, my flesh softening treacherously around me. Blood arrived, like a declaration of guilt.

"What now?" I asked our dad, and he fetched sacking to flatten my chest and wool to soak up my blood. He showed me how to dip a thumb in ash to mask my softness.

"How do you know this?" I asked, and he shook his head, silenced still by sorrow.

My brothers and I each had our time at the lakeside. Mab would go at dusk, his cornflower eyes searching the gloaming for what we'd lost. Brychan would go by moonlight, his freckles dark stars on his skin. I chose dawn, slipping from my clothes and bindings at the water's edge and wading in until I could almost touch her beside me in the chill, clear depths.

Mab was the son who saw her, with whom she shared her wisdom of healing roots and leaves so he could pass them on to us. And Brychan said he heard her in the rustle of rushes and lap of the water; the soft breath of air on its surface.

I felt her skin next to mine, and as my body reformed itself to what must be disguised, she pressed against the pains that came and washed the blood from my flesh, her cheek cool at my temple in sympathy and warning.

*

Cledwyn was one of the village boys who helped us at the farm. I watched him collect eggs with a gentleness that made my insides curl until I needed to turn from him and hide my flushed cheeks. He watched me watching him and held a hand out. I reached mine out in mirror to his and accepted the dusk-blue egg he offered.

It was still warm.

"A duck must have got in without us seeing, Eil," he said, as though that meant something.

I noticed him often then, noticed his calm quiet staring down the farm's fierce cockerel or the worst of the drunks in the pub courtyard.

My brothers cautioned me to be careful.

Mab was almost wed by that point. We bid his days in our shared bed farewell with ale and laughter. His bride blushed crimson from her corner of the courtyard, hearing our lewd talk of the marriage night. I was the worst; I know that, with my empty talk of penetration. I could only conjure what my brothers instinctively understood. I was the worst with the ale also, the stars swaying above me as a confusion of emotions sank in my veins like silt, like grain.

Not man, not woman, not human nor fey, not water nor land, not happy nor sad, but somehow built up of all these things.

Cledwyn accompanied me halfway home.

"I've seen you, Eil," he said suddenly. "I know the truth of your mother, and I know about you."

He confessed to walking early to gather moorhen eggs by the lake, to spying me wading from the water unclothed.

I stared at him, mind stumbling. "Who would believe you?"

"Everyone," he said simply, and touched the heel of his hand to my chin. "But I'll tell none."

He moved into the farm before the moon passed through its cycle, moved into my bed as Brychan made his by the hearth where our dad sat each night. We told the villagers Cledwyn had bought the farm; that he sanctioned us to remain as a mark of compassion.

At Mab's wedding I gazed at his bride with flowers wound in her long hair and ran my fingers over my own shorn scalp. She was aglow in my brother's love and I found myself choking on snot from my tears.

Cledwyn knocked a fist to my chin, hissing, "Get it together, Eil."

His arms around me at night filled me with such contentment that it became a chore to rise before daybreak. When I confessed my reluctance to leave his embrace, he smiled.

"I'll come with you."

We crept together through the dew, and he showed me the beauty of grebes' floating nests; the stippled moorhen eggs; toads' pearled strings of spawn, and damselflies born one thing to become another.

In the water, my mother's approval swam beside me, but through her gladness for my newfound joy I felt her fret about sadness to come.

Before the morning of my niece's baptism, I bled through the clothes I'd slept in and ruined our sheets with my foolish hopes for a child. However much I scrubbed, the emptiness would not fade.

In front of the local gossips, Cledwyn knocked his fist to my temple. "Clumsy clot, to drip my wine over the laundry."

*

I could not loosen my wish for a babe of our own, and at last that want took root. Cledwyn's love beamed over me like firelight. I gave up rising early to go to the lake for fear of my mother's dread blighting our happiness.

For the last few months I stayed indoors. When my son bucked within me, my brothers held me between them, thinking comfort and strength into me until he was born.

I named our child Eirian, meaning bright, meaning beautiful. Our boy had his younger uncle's ash-freckled skin and his elder uncle's cornflower eyes, but it was my spirit I felt blaze from him as I let him suckle on the fullness of my chest one last time.

To keep my secrets safe, Eirian went to live with Mab and his family. Devoted uncle that I was, I visited as often as the farm could spare me, and whispered my truth to him at every chance.

Sickness reached the village. My brothers and I strived to undo its grasp, it bore the old and the young with it, sweeping my father and child into its embrace.

At the funeral, the village gathered to comfort my brother's wife, as he and his children sobbed around the grave. I thought of all my brother had, and the parentage I'd never master. A great, harrumphing laugh burst out of me, grief-laced and skewered with pain.

Cledwyn knocked his fist to my eye. "This life is not for you," he said, and then whispered soft, "This love is not for us."

The lake was waiting. I could feel it in my heart, my bones, my guts, my lungs. I rose at dawn and kissed my brothers goodbye.

Together they trailed me down to the water's edge: cornflower-eyed, ash-freckled behind me. Stepping into the cloud-flooded lake, I felt my mother's touch and knew Cledwyn had done me right.

Carry the Sky

NOT MANY FOLKS are out this afternoon. All it takes is a fine dousing drizzle to keep the dog walkers, cyclists and joggers away, John thinks, half-pitying them, half-glad for the peace their absence affords. In front of him, the river dapples like a thing alive, reflecting fractured pieces of sky. Following the storms, large branches still drift through, faking at being creatures worth pointing out to Amy before sinking out of sight.

They'd seen an eel the afternoon before, dead and sliding with the current like an old piece of tubing. Amy had recoiled, face screwed up. John isn't buying that though. He remembers when she was small, nudging frogspawn with curious fingers. That inquisitive child still has to be in there somewhere.

She's eleven now, Amy, old enough to want to be just about anywhere else when he's charged with keeping an eye on her.

Always bored, that's her trouble. Worse than her mum, Nicki, at that age. At least Amy has that iPod thing to occupy her, fingers always tapping – playing games or sending messages in that strange, abbreviated language – half the letters missing. No wonder she's struggling at school, getting special tuition with her spelling and more.

Her mum never needed extra help at school. John reckons Amy must have inherited her trouble with writing from her dad, Chris. Dyslexic, Nicki told John, not long after she met the lad, dyslexic but determined. And ruthless, when he needed to be, to get on at work. The word ruthless made John wary initially; it seemed to him to be a synonym for heartless. Took him a while to unlearn that, to notice the way Chris was always watching out for Nicki, checking she was safe. More than once he saw the lad move to ensure she was on the inner edge of the path, away from the road with its traffic and grit. A gentleman in both senses of the word. Gentle giant.

Why had it taken him so long to deduce the man's good qualities? He, who prides himself on his ability to read others? John draws up another memory, of seeing Chris standing with Amy at the brink of the stream in Evershot when she was tiny, throwing in twigs to watch them bob towards the sea.

Where'd it come from, dyslexia? No one had it when John was young, though there'd been some kids who'd do no better than the factories. Dyslexia may well have been their trouble, with no diagnosis to help back then.

There, another long word. Diagnosis. When he'd retired, Nicki teased him that he'd lose those, lose his intellect. Particularly when he spent most of his days on a Dorset riverbank, speaking to no man or woman. When in fact what he does here, for hours on end, is twiddle with words, rolling them across his mind like clouds across the sky, dredging up memories of poems he learnt by rote at school. And other memories, recollections as varied as the shades of green in the landscape around him.

They're similar in that way, he and Nicki, blessed with rich inner worlds. John adheres to that idea. Maybe while she lies there, quiet in the curtain-drawn dark of the bedroom she'd shared with Chris, her mind is dancing.

This one, though, restless beside him, she's something else. Won't settle to anything. Even turned her nose up at the prawn mayo sandwich he brought because it used to be her favourite. Nibbled at half, and then stuck it in its wrapper. Nothing's good enough, these days.

"See that, a dragonfly," he says, pointing to the creature as it alights on a reed. "Ferocious predators, those."

He wants her to be interested like she used to be, but she just flicks her lashes and turns back to her screen. As if to say, having to be here is bad enough – don't expect me to speak too.

It irks him. Not like he asked to have his days encroached on by a moody pre-teen. Not like he wanted his Nicki widowed at the age of forty-one, for that matter.

He feels ashamed then. Poor kid, dad felled by an aneurism, mum bed-bound with grief. And what was it Olwyn said in her matter-of-fact way? "Make the most of it, old man. So you don't know how to talk to her – this is your chance to learn."

It's their third day of this; three days into the spring half term. After the first morning he managed to prise the headphones away from her. The skinny threads of wires are still balled up in his pocket. Confiscated.

"Like being at school," she'd scowled, but they hadn't had the raging barney he'd expected. Maybe, as Olwyn suggested, she actually wants to talk, just doesn't know where to start. He ought to try and ease the words out of her.

He used to be good at that kind of thing. Travelled all over for his work as a sociological consultant, always enjoyed that aspect of it – slipping away from the group to find a café, chat to the locals, gauge the real sentiments of the place behind what officials chose to show.

He'd relished the challenge of it, in those days. Never felt he needed more than a smattering of dialect to get by. So much of what was said came through the set of the mouth, flash of the eyes, an almost imperceptible tightening at the shoulders.

He looks at Amy, at the way she slumps on her foldaway chair; drooping like a thirsty gerbera.

"I went to a place once where they'd flooded a valley to make a leisure lake, so holidaymakers would come and fish and kayak and what have you," he says, images of that sun-dazed scenery bouncing in at him. "They covered over a whole village with gallons: houses, shops, church – the lot."

She raises her head, and he's tripped as always by the purpleish-blue of her eyes, the same as her mum's, same as Olwyn's. Identical pair of eyes passed down generation by generation. A bit magical, that, he thinks, as though, perhaps, the things they've seen are passed down too.

"Local government built them a new village on higher ground, an exact replica of the old one," he continues carefully, like he's drawing in a line as smooth as glass, trying to keep the fish on it against all odds.

"Creepy," she sniffs. "Why'd they want it to seem the same?"

"Interesting question!" He's delighted. "Well, why do you think they wouldn't?"

She shrugs, an impatient gesture. "Why pretend? You might forget for a moment, with everything looking the same. Then you'd remember and feel awful all over again."

She meets his gaze for a second, then turns away, dropping her eyes to the gadget's screen once more.

He feels he's made headway, the sense rushing in as it used to when he found the crux of his report and understood how he'd write up what he'd deduced, to hopefully make things better in one corner of the world.

"D'you know, I think they felt exactly that," he says. "You've sussed something not one of the officials uprooting those people from their homes had the empathy to see."

She flushes, as though in recognition of the compliment. *Insightful*, he thinks and grins, wondering how he can turn that to his advantage.

"All right, what do you think we're doing here, day after day? Not us two, *us*." John uses his arm to indicate the row of men who come here; rods arching over the river, low refractive lines designed to be almost invisible in water.

She considers this, accepting the challenge. "It's not about the fish," she says at last.

John nods. Of course it's not. Didn't take three days of sitting to notice how few of them actually caught anything. "What, then?"

She frowns, shrugs. He can feel her slipping off the line. "'cause you're a bunch of loons," she mutters.

He can't help laughing at that, and she looks at him in surprise.

"You might be right, there, kid, you probably are, but there's more to it than that. Come on, give it some thought. What d'you reckon I come here for? It's not just to wind you up, I promise."

She shrugs again, but her face has relaxed its frown.

"Come on, think. What can you see? What can you hear?"

She turns around, and exhales loudly. "Nothing, right? There's nothing here! Just a load of grass and plants and trees and, and ducks! Boring as fu…"

"Amy!" He halts her before the curse escapes her lips. God, to hear that from her mouth. Sometimes he thinks she's still that tiny child intrigued by frogs and toads and ladybirds in equal measure.

She's clammed up, as lost to him as surely as a perch slipping away on the current.

She grips the iPod thing in her hand; scrolling through scenes he catches glimpses of. He swallows his sigh, turning back to the river. This is what he wanted, wasn't it? Plenty of peace and quiet.

He can't stop himself glancing at her surreptitiously, not moving anything but his eyeballs. Her head's down again, hair over her face. Watching something, he thinks.

Suddenly her eyes dart up, catching him staring. He expects an explosion, or at least more sullenness, but she grins.

"Here, take a look at this," she says, holding out the device to him. "Some bloke reckons he saw a crocodile in the river near here. Could that even be true?"

John watches the footage play, showing something long and pale with mottled markings. It rises from the murky water and dips under again. Probably nothing more than a bit of wood swept along by the current, he thinks.

"It's definitely possible," he says slowly. "As much rain as we've had changes a waterway. Things get washed out of storm drains, things that have been hiding."

"Like crocs!" she exclaims, and there she is, the kid he used to know, excited by nature and all its secrets.

"I'm not saying it is one!" he chuckles, passing the machine back to her. "Just saying it's not impossible."

She beams at him, just for a second or two, tops.

It's enough to make him brave. "I know this wasn't what you wanted, spending your half term on the riverbank with an old duffer," he says. "You understand why you're stuck here, don't you?"

The light ebbs from her and he almost wishes he hadn't spoken.

"I'm not thick," she mutters, glowering, then reels off: "Dad died, Mum's in bed, Nan's looking after Mum. You're what's left to me." Her lips pinch in, eyes slits against the thin sunlight that's battling through clouds.

And you're what's left to me, right now, he thinks, although he doesn't really believe it. They sit in silence for a moment, then John coughs, choking down the grief rising in him. "And the crocodile," he says, bright as he can manage. "You, me and the Dorset croc, eh?"

Laughter erupts out of her, wrapped around in her own grief and jagged, jangled, feelings. "Oh, yeah, the crocodile. First one to see it gets the leftover sandwich!"

"And if neither of us does?" he asks, smiling, feeling that in years to come they'll say to one another, *Remember the crocodile? In the river in Dorset?* And no one else will understand why they're bent over laughing.

"Then… then we'll feed it to the ducks," she says decisively.

They sink back into silence, but this time it's a comfortable sort of quiet; just the two of them watching the river slide past, carrying the sky with it.

Acknowledgements

Versions of several of the stories in this collection have previously been published elsewhere. Thanks are due to the editors of these publications.

'Untrue Blue' was published in Bristol Fiction Writers' anthology *A Reimagined Bristol*, and was performed by actor and writer Susan Lavender at Liars League Hong Kong. Susan also performed 'Geese Among the Trees' at Liars League Hong Kong.

'Knotted Rope' was published by Seren Books as their short story of the month in June 2018.

'Two Pools of Water' was published by *Dear Damsels*.

'Apollo's Offspring' was published by *Rathalla Review*.

'The Puppeteer' was published by *Toasted Cheese*.

'Fascinate' was published in the National Flash Fiction Day anthology *Sleep is a Beautiful Colour*.

'Paper Flowers' was published by *The Island Review*.

'Strawberry Thief' was published by *Straylight Magazine*.

'The Moth Room' was published by *Gone Lawn*.

'Far From The Farm' was published as 'The Creak of Snow' by *Literary Orphans*.

'Breaking Up With You Burns Like Fire' was published by *The Drabble*.

'Flamingos and Ham' was published by *Ellipsis Zine Two*.

'Elevated Truths' was published by *Fictive Dream Magazine*.

'Not Every Wound Can Heal' was published by *Spelk Fiction*.

'Little Blessings' was published by *The Germ Magazine*.

'Lodged' was published as 'Unwanted Guests' by *Origami Magazine*.

'Invertebrates' was published by *Door Is A Jar* Magazine.

'Distant Storms' was published in Mslexia's *Little Ms* email newsletter.

'The Sculptor' was published in Unthank Books' *Unthology 8*.

'Underwire' was published by *Tears in the Fence*.

'Breathing Water' was published by *The Skylark Review*.

'Reeds and Curlews' was published as 'Wriggler' by *Ghost Parachute*.

'Fin' was published as part of Micro Madness for National Flash Fiction Day NZ 2018.

'Merrow Cave' was published by *Querty Magazine*.

'Milk and Other Lies' was published by *Smokelong Quarterly*.

'Edge of the Sand' was published by *In The Moment* magazine.

'What Rises' was published as 'The People of the Soil' by *Enchanted Conversation* magazine. The story was inspired by the Welsh myth of the Lady of Llyn y Fan Fach.

Thank you to every friend, family member, author and editor who encouraged me to continue writing, helped me to celebrate the fledgling successes along the way and offered advice that improved my writing in small and large ways.

Thank you to my editor, Tess, for making such clear-eyed suggestions and helping me regard my words with fresh clarity, and to my publisher, Jamie, for bringing this book to life.

Special thanks are due in bucketfuls to my lovely James, my book-loving parents Pauline and Philip, my sister Alice, the friends who have supported me simply through being interested and making an effort to understand my obsessive desire to write, and the writing friends who've helped in other ways, including Elisabeth, Grace, Kevlin, Maithreyi and Zan. Without your patience, feedback and friendship these stories may never have seen the sky, light or rain.

Lightning Source UK Ltd.
Milton Keynes UK
UKHW020617261019
352350UK00005B/147/P

9 781912 436231